the Story of my
LIFE

anne cassidy

... 10 digit ...
... 13 digit ISBN 978 0439 94295 9

... ish Library Cataloguing-in-Publication Data
... record for this book is available from the British Library
All rights reserved

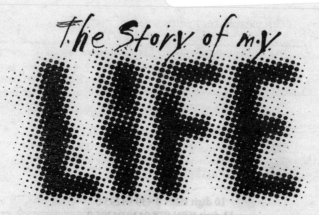

... sold subject to the condition that it shall not, by way of
... se, be lent, hire ... otherwise circulated in any form
... cover other than that in ... is published. No part
... tion may be reproduced, stored in a retrieval system, or
... ed in any form ... any means electronic, mechanical,
... ng, recording ... the prior written
... per... ... holastic Limited.

... Copyright ... anne cassidy Chorion group
... by Richard Hollow

▲SCHOLASTIC

First published in 2006 by Scholastic Children's Books
An imprint of Scholastic Ltd
Euston House, 24 Eversholt Street
London, NW1 1DB, UK
Registered office: Westfield Road, Southam, Warwickshire, CV47 0RA
SCHOLASTIC and associated logos are trademarks and or registered
trademarks of Scholastic Inc.

This edition published by Scholastic Ltd, 2007
Text copyright © Anne Cassidy 2006
The right of Anne Cassidy to be identified as the author of this work
has been asserted by her.

MORAY COUNCIL
LIBRARIES &
INFO.SERVICES

20 26 65 31

Askews

JCY

ISBN 978 0439 04295 9

British Library Cataloguing-in-Publication Data
A CIP catalogue record for this book is available from the British Library.

All rights reserved

This book is sold subject to the condition that it shall not, by way of
trade or otherwise, be lent, resold, hired out or otherwise circulated in any form
of binding or cover other than that in which it is published. No part of
this publication may be reproduced, stored in a retrieval system, or
transmitted in any form or by any means (electronic, mechanical,
photocopying, recording or otherwise) without the prior written
permission of Scholastic Limited

Printed by CPI Bookmarque, Croydon, Surrey
Papers used by Scholastic Children's Books are made from wood grown
in sustainable forests.

3 5 7 9 10 8 6 4

This is a work of fiction. Names, characters, places, incidents and
dialogues are products of the author's imagination or are used fictitiously.
Any resemblance to actual people, living or dead, events or locales is
entirely coincidental.

www.scholastic.co.uk/zone

CONTENTS

ONE
SATURDAY, 17 DECEMBER, 10.42 P.M.

The last thing Kenny Harris wanted was blood on his hands. He almost smiled at this thought. Wasn't it too late to worry about such things? He was in too deep. He couldn't turn back now.

He was standing on Leyton platform. The Central Line. Above him a clock hung like a huge blank face, its hands stuck at three forty. He looked at his mobile to check the time. 22:48. He thought of Nat waiting for him at her house. He imagined himself trying to explain it all to her. The mess he was in. He found the words of an argument playing through his mind. He saw himself appealing to her. *I wasn't always like this*, he would say, his hands out in supplication.

He had to stop. The air was heavy with rain but there wasn't a sound as it hit the ground. The clock stared sullenly and he took a deep breath. He looked down at his bruised hand, his battered jeans, his busted-up trainers. With his good hand he felt above his eyebrow

1

for the cut. It had stopped bleeding but was swollen and sore to touch.

He shivered with the cold. He turned and looked along the track for the glow of an approaching train but there was just a thick slice of blackness. He listened intently for a second. There it was, he was sure, in the distance; the rhythmic clatter of the wheels.

Where are you, Tommy?

The words ran through his head. A couple of people appeared on the platform opposite. A man and a woman, standing silently side by side. Like two ghosts that had come from nowhere.

Tommy Fortune. Where are you?

The man opposite said something to the woman. She turned her head away. In the distance there was the sound of a car braking. A sudden screech that set Kenny's teeth on edge.

He had five, six hours left to find him.

The drizzle turned to rain abruptly. Just like that. It hammered on to the tracks and Kenny stepped back, away from the platform edge, into the dry. He watched the rain spearing down, invisible in the darkness but under the light it shone like steel.

His hand touched the back pocket of his jeans. The letter was there, folded in two. He'd taken days to write it and now it was finished. What would he do with it?

Something fluttered in his stomach. He could walk away. Leave things to sort themselves out. But wouldn't that just make Mack more angry? And make things worse?

His hands were cold. He shoved them into his jacket pockets and grimaced as pain shot through his injured fingers. It made him feel nauseous for a moment. No, worse than that. The shock of the beating came back to him. Being thrown around like a rag doll, punched in the head, kicked in the thigh, his fingers smashed up. From the ground he'd looked up expecting more but there was just the sound of the car pulling away, revving up the road, leaving him like a rubbish bag on the street.

Was he afraid of Mack? Yes, he was. After tonight, Tommy Fortune would be afraid of him as well.

He steeled himself. *Keep calm*. With his good hand he cradled his bruised fingers, his crushed knuckle. If he could just get *warm*.

Looking along the track he saw the distant light of the train. He'd been right, had heard it from miles away. One stop to Stratford and then he would get the Docklands Light Railway to Poplar. It wouldn't take him long. He breathed deeply but felt his chest tightening. He coughed a couple of times and searched around in his pockets for his inhaler. He shook it and frowned. It felt empty. Pretty soon he wouldn't be able to breathe at all. He'd have no choice but to go home. He put it in his mouth and inhaled gently as the train rumbled in filling the platform with yellow light.

He got into the carriage and sat in the first seat

available, his legs splayed. It was almost empty. Just one old bald man sitting in the corner seat, a book open on his lap. He looked over at Kenny, his forehead wrinkling. Kenny turned away. Exactly how bad did he look? The man went back to his book, crossing his legs as if to ward Kenny off.

Kenny made himself focus on the window. They were still above ground. The rain was hitting the glass in darts and he leaned back, feeling the warmth of the carriage, and closed his eyes. After a while he felt the suck of the train as it went back underground.

He got off at Stratford. Like Leyton, the station was above ground and even though it was late the platform was busy. People were standing in groups waiting for overground trains or walking towards the exits to change on to other lines. The platforms were brightly lit up, bathed in the lights from the nearby high-rise buildings. Kenny squinted into the light. He saw the rain turning into snow before his eyes. In the windows of the glass buildings he could see triangles of coloured lights. Christmas trees everywhere. It was all too bright, too cheerful. He turned away and walked briskly towards the darker end of the station where the Docklands Light Railway terminated.

There was one other person standing waiting. A young woman with a baby in a pushchair. When he got closer he could see that she was younger than he'd thought. Fourteen, fifteen maybe. She had hardly any hair and a piercing right in the middle of her top lip. The baby, a toddler, was sound asleep. She gave him a funny look and started to back away, reversing the pushchair. He backed off himself. He must look a fright.

A beeping sound made him turn away. He pulled his mobile out and looked at the screen. Two messages. His fingers were too sore and stiff to press the buttons so he had to use his other hand. It took a minute.

The first message was from Nat. *Where are you? I've waited all night!!!*

The second was from Mack. *Don't forget. By six at the latest. Bring Tommy to the Sugar House.*

He had to find him first.

From out of the dark he saw a square of light. It was small and bright and he could hear the sound of it chugging towards him. The DLR. The train that didn't need a driver. He watched it get bigger and finally trundle into the station. The first time he had travelled on it he had been thrilled. He'd sat at the front as though he, himself, was the driver. How old had he been? Eight, nine? Just a boy.

The doors opened and half a dozen people got off. The girl with the pushchair walked towards the front end and got on. Kenny went to the rear carriage and sat down. He snapped his mobile shut. It lay in his good hand cold and solid. It was brand new, his birthday present from his mum and dad. His birthday, ten days before. A day he wanted to forget. He squeezed his eyelids shut. He would push it away. He would close it up behind some heavy door in his head. His seventeenth birthday. The worst night of his life.

He stared at his reflection in the glass opposite. Ghostly. Ghastly.

The doors of the train closed and a second later it moved off, into the darkness.

TWO
MEETING JIMMY MACKINTOSH

Three months before. September. That was when everything took a turn for the worse. Kenny was coming home from Oxford Street, standing on the Docklands Light Railway platform at Stratford. He was feeling pleased with himself. In his bag were some DVDs he'd been searching for; *Scarface*, *Goodfellas* (special edition) and *French Connection I* and *II* in a boxed set, something he hadn't expected to find. It was just after ten and he was humming to himself, looking forward to getting home and fitting his purchases on to his shelves in alphabetical order. It wouldn't be long, he thought, until he needed to get another set of shelves to house his collection.

It gave him a good feeling.

Kenny turned away from the tracks and saw a familiar face. It was Natalie, his brother's girlfriend. She was at the far end, nearer the bright lights of the main platforms. She was leaning against a post and looked weighed down by shopping bags. At that moment she noticed him and gave a little wave, raising a couple of her bags in the air. She walked in his direction and he felt a little flip in his chest and straightened his belt as he slowly walked towards her.

She was wearing cut-off jeans and a flimsy top. She looked cold. He had an impulse to put an arm around her and warm her up. He dismissed it, pushed it out of his head. She was *his brother's girlfriend* for pity's sake.

"Hey!" she said.

He stood by her, self-conscious, shy for a moment and looked around to avoid eye contact. That was when he noticed a group of lads approaching further along the platform.

"Shopping?" he said, stupidly.

"Got paid today. Thought I'd treat myself. You?"

"Got some DVDs," he said, pointing to his bag.

"Let's see!" she said, brightly.

He pulled them out, holding them like a pack of cards. She picked one out.

"Joe said you liked war type movies," she said, turning it over and reading the back.

"Not *war*," Kenny said, dismissively. "Gangster genre. Mafia, organized crime, that sort of stuff."

"A sort of war, then?" she said, smiling at him, touching his hand lightly when she replaced the DVD. "Good against bad?"

He opened his mouth to argue but then saw that she was teasing him. He swallowed a couple of times and put the DVDs back in their bag.

8

"Not seeing Joe tonight?" he said, stating the obvious.

Why couldn't he think of anything good to say?

"He's working late. You should know. He's your brother!" she said with a little laugh.

Her hair was standing up on her head, as if it had been blown that way. She saw him looking and dropped a couple of her bags and reached up to pat her head.

"I must look a state!" she said.

Kenny didn't answer. For a few seconds he looked straight at her and she didn't look away. She knew she looked good. He could see it in her face, in her direct stare. It was he who lowered his eyes. She was his brother's *girlfriend*. He turned his body away from her and saw, with surprise, that the lads who had been further along the platform were now about ten metres away.

Natalie hadn't seemed to notice but he felt a vague sense of unease. There were three of them, two white and one black. They were about his age, wearing casual stuff, the black kid in an Arsenal shirt. The tall white boy had round glasses on that made him look like a student. Kenny felt a flicker of recognition, as if he knew him from somewhere.

"Joe says you're starting your A levels this year?" Natalie said, oblivious to the change in the atmosphere.

Kenny nodded, keeping the three of them in the corner of his eye. They were looking across at him and he felt a charge in the air and stood as tall as he could.

"I'm in year twelve, I don't know if Joe told you. I'm hoping to go to Bournemouth next year to do American Studies."

"That's interesting," he said, only half aware of what she was saying.

"It means I get to go to the States for a year. Quite crafty of me, really!"

She carried on talking as the three boys started to move in their direction. He glanced down at her and gave polite answers but his attention was elsewhere, a frisson of fear tingling through him. Twisting round he looked along the line, to see if a train was coming. It wasn't. He turned back and was face to face with the tall white kid, who had taken his glasses off. Kenny held his stare for four, five seconds, until the kid blinked and looked away. Natalie had stopped talking and was looking mystified.

"What's the matter?" she said, turning to look at the tall white kid and then back to Kenny.

"Let's move," he said.

He took her elbow and steered her along the platform towards the exit. He wasn't a coward but there were three of them and one of him. Natalie was faffing about with the bags. She was talking on and had no idea what was happening. He tried to hurry her but she was dithering. The black lad sped up and walked across their path, forcing them to stop. Kenny dropped his eyes to the ground and stepped to the side, roughly pushing Natalie along with him. Just ten more steps and they'd be in the bright lights of the main platforms. Just ten steps.

"What's wrong, Kenny? What's going on? I need to get the DLR. . ."

But he had to stop. The white boy who was no longer

wearing his glasses was shoulder to shoulder with him edging him into the wall. He had no choice. He stood still and pushed Natalie on.

"What's the matter?" she said and stood for a moment looking at him and then at the three lads. He could almost see the wheels turning in her head.

He squared his shoulders.

"What?" he said, staring hard at the white boy.

Natalie's face had a puzzled look, a half smile one moment, a frown the next.

"You want this?" he said, shoving his hand in his pocket, pulling out his mobile.

The black kid swore and started to laugh.

Kenny's back was stiff and hard. He gripped his mobile.

"Even my mum's got a better mobile than that!" the white kid said.

"I know you," Kenny said. "You used to go to my school with my brother Joe. You're Jon Tibbs."

"Joe Harris's little brother!" he said. "The kid who thinks he's hard!"

"Don't show me up. I'm with. . ."

Kenny pointed at Natalie.

"She's not bad. Good tits," the black kid said.

Jon Tibbs put his arm around Nat's shoulder and pulled her towards him. Natalie swore and shook him off. They all laughed. Kenny felt himself tighten up, his muscles hardening, his jaw like steel. He looked at Natalie's face, dismayed, confused, holding her clothes-shop bags up to her chest. His eye rested on hers for

11

only a second. It was enough. He sharpened his shoulders and lowered his head, dropping the bag with the DVDs on to the ground. Using every bit of strength he took a sudden lunge at the black kid, ramming him and knocking him over so that he fell backwards on to the platform, his head hitting the concrete.

"Get out, Natalie!"

He hissed and braced himself as Jon Tibbs jumped on his back and forced him down on to the ground, smacking his face on to the concrete. He closed his eyes and steeled himself as a ball of pain exploded in his side and then another. They only had trainers on but each kick seemed to be steel-capped. He could hear Natalie squealing and shouting but her words were far away, too far away to be of any help. Three against one. The black kid was still lying on the ground and Kenny reached out and grabbed his face, using his fingers he searched out the boy's eyes, trying to do damage. He felt his shoulders wrenching back, though, as the other two dragged him along the platform into the blackness, away from the light. Nat's cries were like whispers in the back of his head.

"Oi!"

A voice cut through the darkness. Loud and insistent. Kenny slumped on to the ground, no longer being dragged or held.

"You! Leave him alone. Leave that lad alone."

He turned his face and saw some polished shoes marching in his direction. Dark trousers with creases. He should make an effort to get up, make the most of the distraction, but the pain in his sides was eating away at him, taking great bites out of his ribs.

He saw the feet of the two white kids moving away. All the time they were swearing and shouting at the man with the smart trousers. Kenny saw them pick their mate up off the ground and pass Natalie as she came running back up the platform followed by a small man in a London Transport uniform. He saw a hand extended in his direction.

"Let me help you up, mate."

He allowed the man to help him up, his legs feeling like elastic bands.

"You're in a bit of mess," he said.

He had a suit jacket on with an open-necked shirt. He wasn't old, maybe twenty-five. There was a low rumble in the distance. It distracted Kenny. A train.

"I'm all right," he mumbled, embarrassed now.

He wasn't all right. His sides were on fire and when Natalie reached him she put her arm around his waist to help steady him. He had to lean on her to walk and he tried to focus through the stream of complaints she was making to the Underground worker, her voice shrill.

"I'll take you to the hospital, if you like," the man said.

In the background the London Transport man was backing away.

"No, I'll just go home," said Kenny. "It's just a couple of bruises."

"I don't think so, mate. You look pretty roughed up to me."

The train came in, lighting the platform up. The man

turned and walked back up the platform, bent down to pick something up and came back towards him. The train doors opened and a couple of people got out. Kenny edged Natalie on. The man handed him his bag of DVDs.

"I could travel with you. Just in case. . ."

"I'm all right. Thanks. . ."

"No problem. My name's Jimmy Mackintosh. People call me Mack."

"Thanks," Kenny said and stepped on to the train, his elbow clamped against his side, holding his ribs as still as he could. The carriage was empty and he sat down in the first seat he could. Nat gave the man a wave as the doors closed.

"Thank God he came along!" she said, sitting beside him, her face scrunched up with fright and worry, her eyes still red from crying.

It was his first meeting with Mack. There were more to come.

THREE

At Poplar Kenny headed for the Scarlet Lady, one of Tommy Fortune's regular haunts. The only other place he could think of was Jack's All-Nite Café but that was a long walk or possibly a cab ride away.

Tommy Fortune wasn't usually so hard to find. He was always turning up somewhere. Now that Kenny was looking he was nowhere to be found. He pulled his jacket tight and walked down the steep stairs from the DLR station. He glanced over to his left and saw the giant office blocks of Canary Wharf. Just two minutes from West India Quays where the all-night club the Sugar House was. It gave him a bad feeling just looking in that direction. He turned away and walked towards the high street.

What he really wanted to do was to go home. To go up to his room, close the door, maybe even lock it, lie down on his bed and pull the duvet right over his head.

The rain had softened but it felt icy on his face. He

pulled his collar up. Maybe it would snow properly. That was something nice. The streets covered in a layer of white. First thing in the morning when it was pristine. A pretty world in which bad things didn't happen.

Up above, the DLR continued rolling. From where he was it looked like a giant fairground ride. The lit-up carriages waddled away along the line, disappearing against the background of the office blocks, reappearing only where they were silhouetted against the black sky.

Kenny pushed his chin into his jacket and strode on. His thigh hurt him whenever he put weight on it. He stopped and rubbed at it, pushed his foot hard on to the ground, moved it from right to left. It still felt the same. He'd have to try and ignore it. A police car siren sounded nearby and it startled him for a moment. He looked guiltily around and then walked on. On the high street there was still some traffic queuing. He wondered whether people were just going out or on their way home. In the distance he could see the pub, the Scarlet Lady, its bright lights shining out.

His brother Joe had worked there the previous summer. That's how Kenny knew it. And it was the first place that he'd ever seen Tommy Fortune. He walked gingerly on, passing small groups of people, keeping alert in case Tommy Fortune was among them. At the door of the pub he looked in. The place was packed. There might be some people he knew in there, from school maybe, or some of Joe's old mates. He walked in and the heat and noise hit him. He stood for a moment glancing round, as if he'd arranged to meet someone there and was looking for them. Then he went up to the bar. It was elbow to elbow. After a long wait a blonde woman turned to him. She had a tight top on and her breasts ballooned out of it.

"Yep?" she said, not even looking at him.

He bought a bottle of beer and walked to the far end of the pub. There was a small disco and a raised stage. Its lights were flashing different colours in time with the music. In front was a dance floor the size of his living room. He'd been there with his mate Russell last summer. They'd gone in, pretending they were older, his brother Joe selling them bottles of beer, telling them to keep to the corners, not to make a show of themselves. He was still under-age now but no one would know. He looked older than his years. Some people thought he looked older than his brother.

There was no sign of Tommy. He moved around and then leaned against a wall that gave him a good view of most parts of the pub. Over by a closed-up piano were a couple of familiar faces. Men that he had seen with Tommy. He sighed. If he could just go over and ask them, *Where's Tommy?* How easy it would be. But he didn't want to do that. Mack had been quite clear.

Don't let anyone know you're looking for Tommy. No witnesses. And we don't want any of his mates tagging along. Wait till he's on his own. Then bring him down to the Sugar House. By six. No later.

"Little Kenny!" someone said, smacking him on the shoulder.

17

Kenny turned to face a giant of a man. It was Big Trevor, a pub regular.

"Hi," he said.

"What's happened to you?" he said. "Fighting over a girl?"

Kenny shrugged. Joe had introduced him to Big Trevor when he first worked at the pub. *This is my kid brother,* he'd said and Trevor had roared approval. *He'll have to fight the ladies off, Joe!* he'd said. Trevor's conversation was full of references to girls or ladies.

"That looks bad, maybe needs a couple of stitches," he said, pointing at Kenny's forehead.

"It's fine," Kenny said, drinking from his bottle. Big Trevor pointed to it.

"Plastic bottles now," he said. "Too many fights in here for glass."

Kenny looked at the bottle of beer. Trevor was right. It was plastic. He glanced over to the area near the piano. The familiar faces he had seen were still there. Friends of Tommy. Maybe it was a good sign. Maybe Tommy was due to come in.

"How's Joe? Still trying to change the world?" Big Trevor said.

"Fine." Kenny coughed, the smoky atmosphere getting to his chest. "Still at Durham University. Second year."

"He'll go far," said Big Trevor. "Well, he has already. Durham's a fair distance!"

Trevor laughed a giant's laugh and gave Kenny a heavy-handed pat on the shoulder. "I'll bet he's a hit with the ladies!"

Kenny *ummed* in a noncommittal way. The sound of the disco increased suddenly and a Christmas song came on. A number of people started singing and a group of girls staggered on to the tiny dance floor. Big Trevor's eyes were drawn to the sight and Kenny used it as a chance to slip away. He walked across the pub and stood near the piano, his beer bottle up to his mouth. He recognized three of the people there. They'd been with Tommy the first night he'd met him. When was that? June? Six months ago.

That's Tommy Fortune, Joe had said. *Sells knock-off gear. He's always got cheap DVDs and he sells a bit of dope and anything else he can get his hands on. He's harmless enough.*

Kenny hadn't actually spoken to Tommy that night. He'd looked him over though. He was a thin man wearing a formal suit, with a shirt and a dicky bow. He looked out of place in the pub. How old was he? Mid-thirties? He was already losing hair from the front, which made his forehead look huge.

But tonight he wasn't here. Kenny tried to listen in to what Tommy's mates were saying but the pub was too loud. He put his hand up to his forehead. It felt hot and swollen. Really he needed some painkillers, some ice to cool it, a lie down. The noise and the smoke were getting to him. He wondered how Joe had stuck the job for so long. And he was supposed to be working here over Christmas. Kenny wondered, after all the trouble of the last few weeks, if Joe would be able to do it.

Whatever.

Kenny had his own problems.

He put his bottle down and zipped his jacket up. Then he stepped outside the pub and plunged into the thin, cold air.

FOUR
SATURDAY, 17 DECEMBER, 11.37 P.M.

Nat's house was a short walk from the pub. In a few minutes he was turning into her road. He'd already sent her a text to tell her to expect him. She'd be waiting, he knew, at her back door, her mum and dad already tucked up in bed.

He hugged himself as he walked through the freezing air. There was music coming from one of the houses further up. A party. People enjoying themselves. He paused for a moment, feeling drawn towards the noise. To be able to slip into a group of people and forget himself. If only it were that simple. He turned away and went into the side path at Nat's house and headed for the gate that led to the back garden. He quietly unlatched it and crept in, locking it behind him. The kitchen door was ajar. Peeping out was Nat.

"Come on!" she whispered, impatiently.

He went into the dark kitchen and closed the door.

When he turned back she had her arms around his neck and was kissing him. The room was warm and she felt hot and sleepy. She had a flimsy nightie on that came down to her knees. Underneath she had nothing on, he could feel that. It stirred a desire in him and he pulled her close for a moment.

"Not here!" she said, breaking off the kiss, pulling him by his bad hand towards the hallway.

He cried out and she stopped. She put the light on and looked at him, her face dropping.

"What's happened?" she said, in a loud whisper. "You've been in a fight! Not with Joe?" she said.

He shook his head. He hadn't set eyes on his brother since his birthday. He almost smiled. How funny that Nat should think Joe would do this. Kenny wished Joe had. He wished his brother was the type that would resort to violence.

"You smell of smoke. Have you been in a pub? Is that where the fight was?"

He didn't answer. Let her think what she wanted.

"Were you with that Jimmy Mackintosh?"

"Nat, leave it. I just got into an argument."

"Look at the state of you. I'll have to fix it."

"I need some cash. I have to get a cab. I've got to meet someone. . ." he said, allowing himself to be pulled along the hallway and up the stairs.

Nat put her finger on her lips as she opened the bathroom door and took some things from the wall cupboard. She needn't have bothered telling him to be quiet. He knew her parents would be asleep in the loft

22

bedroom. He'd crept up and down those stairs enough times in previous weeks.

Armed with cotton wool and TCP Nat ushered him along the hallway to the back of the house and her bedroom. Only the bedside light was on and the room was virtually dark.

"Nat, I need some money. Twenty, thirty quid, something like that."

She clucked her tongue and gave him a disapproving look.

"Look at you! Your head and your hand. Anything else?"

"My leg. It's just bruised. It's painful though. Some paracetamol would help. . ."

She manoeuvred him on to the bed and went out of the room. He slumped back. On top of everything else he felt tired. A great heavy weariness was sucking him down. He turned his face into her pillow. A strong smell of scent hit him. He breathed it in, tried to calm himself. Five . . . ten minutes later Nat reappeared and he pulled himself up. She had a glass of water and a mug of something hot.

"Have these," she said, showing him two tablets in her palm.

He swallowed both together.

"Then drink this while I clean you up. It's sweet tea. You need it if you've had a shock."

He did what he was told. Here, in this room with Nat, he could just be a patient. He smelled the TCP as she tipped it on the cotton wool and felt the vicious

23

sting as she wiped it gingerly over the wound on his forehead. He must have made a sound because she said sorry two or three times. She paused while he drunk his tea in great gulps. He was level with her chest. Through the fabric he could see the shape of her tiny breasts. His hands stirred. He wanted to touch her, to put his arms around her and pull her to him so that he could bury his face in her tissue-thin nightie.

"This should stop it bleeding," she said, fixing a plaster over the cut. "But it needs stitches, I think. What about your hand?"

He held his hand close to his chest and shook his head.

"Let me see," she said, pulling it towards her.

He let her open his palm and straighten his fingers. He gasped at the pain.

"You've got to go to the hospital," she said.

"I will, I will. There's somewhere I've got to go first. Someone I've got to see! That's why I need the money?"

"I've got about eight quid in my purse. That's all!" she said, exasperated.

Why was nothing ever simple?

"You can have my cashcard. I'll write my PIN down!" she said.

"I'll go home. I've got money there. I need my inhaler anyway."

"Let me bandage this. And get you some ice for your head. You don't have to rush."

24

She went out and returned with a bandage and a bag of frozen peas wrapped in a tea towel.

"I'm not a nurse," she said, "but I think we should just keep your hand flat . . . and you could just lie down for a while with this on your head. Give the painkillers time to work."

She wound the bandage round his hand, tightly so that he couldn't flex his fingers or make a fist. Then she helped him take off his trainers. He took his mobile out and put it on the chest of drawers beside the bed. She patted the pillows for him and sat beside him on the bed. He pulled her down to kiss her but she shook her head. He lay back on the bed, his head on her pillow.

"You relax," she whispered.

"Just five minutes," he said, closing his eyes, feeling the darkness like a blanket over him.

She said a few more things and he ummed but all the time he knew he was slipping away, his eyelids like two closed doors. He eventually lost his hold on Nat and the room and fell asleep.

Natalie got off the bed. She'd forgotten to use the frozen peas. She left them on the bedside table. Then she pulled the edge of the duvet back and draped it across Kenny's body. She put her fleecy dressing gown on, tied it tight and sat in the armchair by the window.

He'd been fighting. Why didn't it surprise her? He'd been argumentative and moody ever since the day of his birthday. Natalie chewed at her lip and bowed her

25

head. Memories of that day could still make her stomach drop, her goose pimples rise with embarrassment. It must be the same for Kenny, no, worse for him. That's why he was so difficult. How long had it been? Nine . . . ten days? Would things ever get back to normal? She felt restless and stood up, stretching her arms up to the ceiling. She tidied the things she'd used on his injuries, the cotton wool, TCP, plasters, the half-drunk mug of tea. She put them on her desk and looked at the clothes that were hanging over the back of her chair. Her clean jeans and a brand-new top that she'd bought that day. Gold with a line of sequins around the neck. It was strappy and low so she couldn't wear a bra. It was completely unsuitable for winter but she'd wanted it anyway. When she got home from the shops she'd bathed and got herself ready for him. The gold top making her cold, making her nipples stand out.

She sat down in the chair again and sighed. A couple of weeks ago he would have liked it. Now though, since telling Joe the truth, things were different. She'd hardly seen him. He'd spent a lot of time out with his mates, he said. Some of it with Jimmy Mackintosh, she was sure. How long would things take to get back to normal?

She looked out of the window at her side. The rain was turning to snow. She could see it in the garden lights. Six coloured lanterns on the apple tree. Her dad put them up every Christmas. The snow wasn't on the ground though, just in the air. Only seven days until Christmas Day.

Maybe it would stay cold enough to snow then. That way their first ever Christmas together would be a white one.

Kenny was sound asleep, his chest rising and falling, the rest of him still and lifeless. Just looking at him gave her an ache in her ribs. How stupid was that? They'd been together almost nine weeks, most of that in secret. He was everything she should have avoided. He was a year younger for a start. A school drop-out. A troublemaker. He had no plans for the future, no strategy. He was the opposite to her in just about every way she could think.

But when he turned his eyes on to her she felt her skin ripple. Just a boy he was, but when he kissed her her spine seemed to turn to liquid. He took her from Joe. Just like that. Casually and with a smile he turned his gaze on to her and she was drawn towards him. It was as if she had no choice.

She should have felt guilty, but she didn't.

Her friends had been appalled. In the library, when they were all sitting at computer monitors, typing out essays for sociology or English, or notes on history, they made their feelings clear.

"He's a kid!"

"He's a loser!"

"Does his mum still give him pocket money?"

"I'm eighteen! He's only a year younger than me!" she'd said, indignantly.

But girls were meant to go out with older lads, so that made Kenny two or three years too young for her. Unlike Joe, his older brother, who had been about the right age. Joe and Nat, the *perfect* couple.

"He's your boyfriend's brother!" they said, disapprovingly. It was an argument that dwarfed everything else.

But it wasn't always possible to pick the person you fell in love with.

Once Joe found out about them everything blew apart. Kenny's parents wouldn't have her around the house. Her parents were furious that she'd lied to them. Joe's friends had blanked her and some kids at school were whispering behind her back and calling her a slag.

Kenny had faded away from her. At first she thought she'd lost him but in the end he came back. Something was different about him, though. Even his appearance had altered. The truth was he looked ill a lot of the time. Now this. He'd got into a fight. Cheating on his own brother had left him feeling wretched, she understood that. She felt awful.

But it was just a matter of time before things started getting better, she was sure. She chewed at her lip and looked over towards her desk at the gold top hanging limply over the chair, its sparkle dulled in the dim room. On the top of the desk her eye rested on a blue envelope poking out from under her papers. She huffed, got up and plucked the letter from her desk and sat down again. Kenny murmured and turned over in his sleep, pulling his knees up. It startled her and she held the letter guiltily for a moment in case he was about to wake up. Then, when she was sure he was asleep, she pulled the paper out of the envelope. She'd had it for days and not known what to do with it.

Dear Natalie, it said.

Now Joe was calling her *Natalie*, as if she was some kind of distant aunt, not his ex-girlfriend. *We have to talk. You owe me that much. I have to know what happened and why. I'm coming back from uni next Saturday for Christmas and I hoped we could meet. Just to have a talk. Think it over. Yours, Joey. PS I still love you.*

She shook her head. Joe and Nat. Kenny and Nat. Why couldn't she have fallen for a lad with no brothers at all? How simple life would have been.

Kenny woke with a start. He immediately remembered where he was. He turned and looked at the clock. 00:37. He'd been asleep for almost an hour. He had to move. He had to get going. The room was chilly. He sat up. With his good hand he pulled his trainers on. Nat was slumped in the armchair opposite, her bare feet poking out the bottom of her dressing gown. He pulled at the duvet, gathering it up. She made a groaning sound and he paused, not wanting to wake her up. Then he covered her with the duvet.

He felt a bit better. The pain in his leg wasn't so bad and his head didn't feel so hot. The paracetamol had worked. He had to go home though, and get some money. His mum and dad would be asleep and he could slip in and out. He put his jacket on, taking care with his bandaged hand. Turning, he saw a scarf of his hanging on a peg on the back of the door. He must have left it on one of his visits. He took it off and wound it round his neck so that the top of it covered his mouth.

29

For a second he felt brighter, as though the scarf was a good omen of some sort, protecting him from the cold.

Then he remembered Mack's words. *Bring him here. Six o'clock. It's quiet then. I'll have a word with him, put the frighteners on him.* But it wasn't a word Mack wanted. Kenny knew what would happen. He'd had a taste of it himself, earlier that evening.

Tommy Fortune was going to get a beating.

Kenny faltered for a moment, grabbing the handle of the door. *How could he do this?*

After a minute he went out, closing Nat's door quietly behind him. Then he went down the stairs, hardly breathing so as not to wake anyone up.

Natalie woke up. Her head felt heavy, as though she'd been in a deep sleep. Moments later she heard the click of the back door below her bedroom window. She pulled the net curtain back but there was only darkness. She tutted to herself. He should have woken her up. She stood up stiffly, the duvet dropping back on to the floor. She pulled it towards the bed and saw, on the bedside chest of drawers, Kenny's mobile. He must have taken it out of his pocket when he'd lain down. She picked it up and saw a message icon on the screen. It was a voicemail that had been left just minutes before. A gruff male voice. She guessed immediately who it was and the voice irritated her: Jimmy Mackintosh.

Kenny, you listen to me. Don't you let me down. Six o'clock. The Sugar House. Otherwise it'll be bad.

She put the mobile back on her bedside table. That

stupid bloke Mackintosh. Some little scheme or other that he was trying to get Kenny into. Whatever. He would have to wait until tomorrow when she could give Kenny his mobile back.

She turned her bedside light off and lay in the dark.

FIVE
SUNDAY, 18 DECEMBER, 12.59 A.M.

It was a long walk home. The streets were almost empty. Kenny passed a handful of late-night people, partygoers or just tired friends who didn't have the money for a cab. The pavements were wet but the icy rain had stopped. The parked cars glistened with droplets and the street-lights picked out oily puddles on the road. The shop shutters were down but Christmas tree lights still glowed through the windows above. In the middle of the high street there was a giant tree with lights strung across it and a neon sign above that said *Happy Christmas!*. It was almost as bright as daylight. Kenny only gave it a sideways glance, walking slowly, taking care not to put too much weight on his bad leg.

After fifteen minutes or so he took a short cut through the car park of a supermarket and then along a lane that sided on to his school. He was glad of his scarf. It was a pity he hadn't left a hat at Nat's as well. He shoved his good hand in his jeans pocket and pulled out a packet of Polos. He edged the silver paper back and took a couple and popped them in his mouth.

He was feeling better. He looked at his watch. It was a quarter past one. He had hours to go before six o'clock. There was every chance that he'd find Tommy Fortune. Something occurred to him. Maybe *he* could sort things out with the man. Explain to him about Mack. Maybe there would be no need for a meeting down at the Sugar House.

The lane was silent, his footsteps making no sound on the uneven paving stones. On one side were the back gardens of houses. On the other sat the school playing fields. He was completely alone.

He realized then that he couldn't talk to Tommy. If he mentioned Mack's name then Tommy would scarper. The plan wouldn't work. Tommy would never go down to the Sugar House with him. He had to make up a story that didn't involve Mack.

It was a complicated situation.

He looked at the school fields. An expanse of darkness. There were no lights and he could just make out gloomy shapes and masses. When he was younger, still at primary school, he'd spent long evenings creeping in and out of the Big School to play football or generally snoop around. In those days it had been easy, the wire fence dotted with holes. He and his best mate Russell, squeezing through the gaps, ignoring the shouting of the older kids, avoiding the eagle eye of the caretaker. Once or twice they got into the school buildings and wandered round the classrooms.

Simple days. Trespassing in the Big School seemed like a major crime. Excitement had raced through his veins as he ran across the grass, ducking in behind bushes or lying flat out on the pitch hoping to disappear on the horizon. Like soldiers they were, on a mission. He and Russell. Best mates.

Now the school was more secure. A strong, high fence and CCTV cameras that sat like stiff birds on the corners of the buildings. In any case he was a student now. He was allowed into the building.

And these days his *crimes* were more serious.

At the end of the playing fields he turned out of the lane into a street of houses. He speeded up and walked past the school gates, eyeing the sign that said, *East Poplar High School*.

After weeks of not going to school, a letter had arrived the day before telling him he had an interview on Monday with Mr Mullins, the Deputy Head. About his *future*. His mum and dad had insisted he go. Mr Mullins was a quiet-spoken man who had never taught him but had often been around when Kenny was in trouble. He had taught his brother maths for three years. Whenever he was up in front of him Mr Mullins's voice always seemed to drop to a whisper and Kenny would hear how different he was to his brother. How *very disappointing* it was for him that the older Harris was so academic, so much a part of the fabric of the school whereas the younger Harris was just a *waste of space*. Joe Harris; great debater, stalwart member of school drama productions, member of the chess club, took four A levels and got stunning results. When they were kids they'd been close. But once at secondary school Joe turned into some kind of saint. When Kenny joined him, two years later, there were unspoken expectations. Could Kenny live up to Joe's achievements? He didn't even try. He hung round with the difficult lads and his older brother became an embarrassment to him.

Not much had changed.

Joe got a place at a good university and was repeating his success there. His results were good and he was active in the student union. Kenny wasn't impressed. The only thing Joe had ever done that impressed Kenny was to bring Natalie Franks home. *Meet my girlfriend*, he'd said and for a moment, Kenny had been speechless.

Telling Joe the truth about him and Nat had been much harder than he'd thought. He'd expected anger, fury, outrage even. He'd clenched his fist when saying the actual words, *Me and Nat have been together for a while. It started after you went back to uni. She was lonely*. He was ready for Joe to leap up, kick the kitchen chairs out of the way and punch him hard on the nose. He stood, his muscles tense, his feet apart, ready to defend himself.

Joe didn't move. He sat down at the kitchen table and cried. Just remembering it made Kenny's stomach feel nauseous. *You've slept with Nat?* he had said, his words quivering. *How could you? You miserable bastard.*

Reaching the far side of the school Kenny tried to push it out of his mind. Thinking about it upset him.

35

The trouble was that there were other things in his head that were much worse. If only he could put his mind on a kind of "hold". At least until this night was over. He needed his wits about him, but he didn't need his memories and worries crowding in on him. If he could close those bits of his brain down and just run on a kind of autopilot.

He turned towards the better end of the area, Bow, the squares of old houses where his family lived. He paused for a moment, feeling breathless. He needed his inhaler. A car turned into the street, its lights sweeping across him. He blinked and then shielded his eyes. The car slid slowly past. He could hear the music from inside, something light and old-fashioned. A man was driving, one hand up to his ear, talking into his mobile.

Kenny patted his jacket pocket and frowned. He'd left his mobile at Nat's. He swore. He couldn't go back. Not now. He'd have to use his old mobile. There was bound to be some time left on it.

He should get home. Get on with finding Tommy Fortune. Get the whole horrible business over with. He increased his pace and turned the corner into his street and stopped dead in his tracks. Joe's red Ford was parked outside the house. He hadn't expected him home from uni until early next week. He swore. He walked to the car. In the back window there was a sticker: *Make Poverty History*. Kenny rolled his eyes. Standing close he felt a faint whiff of heat coming from it. Joe had only just got here, maybe even in the last half an hour or so. He took a few shallow breaths. He needed to go indoors even though he didn't want to come face to face with him. He needed money and he had to get his inhaler and his old mobile. He put his key in the lock. It was the middle of the night. Maybe Joe had gone straight upstairs to bed.

But when the door opened his brother was there, in the hall, opening letters, staring straight at him.

SIX

"All right?" Kenny said.

Joe gave him a curt nod.

Kenny walked past him straight towards the kitchen. He needed a hot drink. On the hob was a pan of water bubbling away. Beside it was a packet of pasta and a jar of sauce. He felt hungry all of a sudden.

"What happened to you? Were you in a fight?"

Joe's voice came from behind. Kenny ummed. He kept forgetting the way he looked.

"Are you OK?"

"I'm fine. It's just a scratch," he said, without turning round.

"Do you want some food? There's plenty," Joe said.

Without turning round Kenny shook his head and filled the kettle. How could Joe be so polite? Asking questions as though nothing had happened? Kenny got a mug and a sachet of soup out of the cupboard. He should *say* something to his brother, just to be sociable.

38

"Just got here?" he said.

Joe nodded.

"Half an hour or so. Four hours down the M1. M25, M11 and then the A406. Put my foot down in Durham and never stopped till I got here."

Kenny nodded. Just two brothers passing the time having a late-night snack. That's all it was. He watched as Joe turned to the packet of pasta and measured some out. He was thin. His hair was longer and he looked more like a hippie than usual. Around his wrist there were rubber bangles, all in different colours, all making some political point. Even when Joe was heartbroken he still cared about the poor or the homeless or the exploited workers of the Third World.

It was ten days since he'd told him. He would still be upset, Kenny would have bet money on it.

"Been round Natalie's?" Joe suddenly said.

Kenny nodded, his throat tightening. They weren't going to talk about it! Not now.

"How is she?"

"OK."

"How's school?"

"Fine," Kenny said. "What is this, the third degree?"

"Just asking," Joe said, turning round, his hands in mid-air as if to say, *Don't jump down my throat!*

Kenny felt a stab of guilt. Joe was making an effort. Couldn't he, at least, be civil? The kettle had boiled and he poured water on to the powdered soup in his cup. He stirred it vigorously. There was an instant smell of chicken.

39

"I've got a careers interview on Monday."

Loosely speaking it was the truth.

"Uni?" Joe said.

Kenny shook his head. Education, education, education. Having a deputy head for a dad and a teacher for a mum meant that it was a constant topic in his family. How often he had wished his dad was a plumber or a taxi driver. Just so that every conversation about his future didn't include the word "university".

"Not everyone has to go. . ." Joe said, his voice falling at the end.

Disappointment. It hung in the air when he was at home. He was supposed to be like Joe. A high achiever. The fact that he wasn't was always put down to other things. The wrong teacher, the wrong syllabus, peer pressure or stress. He wasn't allowed simply to fail like other people.

"I have to go," Kenny said.

He picked his cup up. *Money, mobile, inhaler*. He was making a list in his head of things he had to get.

"Thing is. . ." Joe said, "it might be good to clear the air. About Natalie."

Kenny felt a squirming sensation in his chest. Not now. Not tonight.

"If you and Natalie are serious. . ." Joe said.

"I can't talk about this. I've got to go, I'm due to meet someone. . ."

"Now? At this time?" Joe said.

"You sound like Mum!"

Joe's face hardened. For pity's sake! What did he

expect? The pair of them to hug like they did on *Friends*?

Joe turned back to the bubbling pot, his shoulders twitching. Kenny started to say *Sorry*, but then thought how ridiculous it would sound.

"I need my inhaler," he said.

Joe didn't speak. He picked the pot up and took it to the sink and poured the water away. In seconds he was enveloped in steam.

Upstairs, Kenny picked up his blue inhaler and sucked the drug into his lungs. He counted up to thirty in his head before he did it for a second time. Then he sat back against his pillows and tried to breathe normally. He knew that in a few moments his lungs would feel looser and he would be able to breathe properly, to get the air down to the bottom of his tubes. It would give him energy. He forced himself to sit still and drink all the chicken soup before anything else. He had to blow on it and sip carefully because it was boiling. It warmed up his throat and made his lips hot.

He looked at the shelves which held his DVDs. Three of them, full up with movies he'd collected and watched. When other people were doing their homework or reading a book he was watching Tarantino or Scorsese. There were movies there he knew by heart, key scenes and important speeches.

It was what he liked. Not Shakespeare or Pythagoras, not like Joe. He was a completely different kind of person.

Finishing his soup he swung his legs off the bed. In

his bedside drawer there were three ten-pound notes and some coins. He put them in his pocket. He grabbed his old mobile. He pressed the *ON* switch and was relieved to see that it had a fair bit of battery.

He heard some movement from next door. His mum or dad getting up to go to the toilet. Then there was the sound of padding feet and a tiny knock on the door.

"Come in," he said, reluctantly.

His mum's head appeared, her hair sticking up to one side as though she'd been lying on the other ear. Her face fell when she registered his plasters and bandage.

"Kenny, what's happened?" she said, sweeping into the bedroom.

"It's nothing. Just a row in a pub. I've been to the hospital," he lied.

"Are you sure? That cut looks bad," she said. "Surely it needs stitches?"

"It's all right."

She looked unconvinced. He turned away from her and pretended to look in his bedside drawer.

"Is that Joe downstairs?" she said.

He ummed.

"Maybe you and him can talk," she said, sitting on the edge of his bed.

"Me and him are all right."

She nodded but her face was full of disbelief. She looked like she had something to say, the words puffing up her cheeks.

"Have you been at that *Natalie's*?"

He didn't answer. His mum blamed Nat for everything.

It was easier that way. Nat was a girl with a shallow heart and loose morals. She would do the same thing to Kenny that she had done to Joe. Kenny would have to look after his own emotional welfare. She was poison and was not allowed in their house.

"I can't talk now. I've got to go out," Kenny said, standing up, hoping to shift his mum from his room.

"Now? In that state? Look at your hand. Who on earth did that bandage?"

"I need to see someone."

"Is it that Macky lad? He called just before I went to bed."

"He phoned here?"

"No, he called at the door. He was looking for you. Said you had something to give him? He said to tell you he was waiting? I was just in my dressing gown. I have to say it was a bit late."

Kenny went to the hooks on the back of his door and grabbed a hooded sweatshirt. He put it on, taking care while slipping his injured hand into the sleeve. His mum got up and helped him.

"Mum!" he said, in a loud whisper.

He pulled his jacket on and picked up his old mobile and his inhaler.

"It's the middle of the night. Dad won't be happy with you going out in that state! Do you want me to give you a lift somewhere? Or Joe could. . ."

"Mum, I'm all right. I'm not going far. . ." he said, opening his room door.

"Zip your jacket up!"

43

He heard her words from behind as he ran down the stairs and went straight out of the front door.

Mack had been here. Mack was waiting for him. He'd been distracted with Nat and Joe. He needed to focus. He had one important job and that was to find Tommy Fortune. He put his head down against the icy night air, and walked towards the station where he knew there was an all-night minicab.

SEVEN
MEETING MACK AGAIN

Kenny had his cashcard in one hand, his wallet in the other. He was waiting behind a woman outside a building society. The sun was beating down on his back and he was squinting. His sunglasses lay on the hall table at home. He'd meant to put them in his pocket but had forgotten.

There were two cashpoints and he was staring at the backs of two men. One was tall, with shorts and a sleeveless top. His tan suggested that he'd just come back from holiday. The other was shorter and had on a West Ham away shirt and faded jeans. The tanned man finished first and the woman in front of him shuffled over, her card in hand, ready to use the machine. The man in the football shirt took another minute or so and Kenny huffed quietly to himself. He had places to go, didn't he? The man finished suddenly and with only a half turn he walked away stuffing his money into his wallet. Something dropped as he headed off. Kenny stepped forward and picked it up. It was a cashcard.

"Oi!" he shouted, taking a step forward and then back, not wanting to lose his place at the cashpoint.

The man continued walking though, and Kenny glanced at the two or three people waiting and the empty cashpoint and the disappearing back of the West Ham fan. He couldn't just let him go. He sprinted off, through the shoppers and got up to the man just as he was joined by another.

"Mate?" he said, in a raised voice. "Mate? I think you dropped your cash—"

The man turned round, his shoulders squared as if he was ready for a fight. Kenny was holding out the card in mid-air. The man looked at the card, and then at Kenny and then back to the card. His face broke into a smile. He swore and plucked the card from Kenny's fingers. He looked familiar. Kenny knew him, he was sure.

"I know you," he said.

"I know you too," the man said. "I know him," he said, giving his mate a shove.

Kenny remembered.

"You were on the DLR platform," he said. "The other week. When I was having a bit of trouble."

Actually it had been almost three weeks before. Kenny pictured the man standing in his suit, looking like a solicitor or a bank manager, his voice startling the kids who were giving him a beating. He'd been embarrassed at the time but grateful all the same.

"You recovered?" the man said, and before Kenny could answer he turned to his mate and said, "This kid, right? He was getting a real going over. Three against one. Not very good odds."

"Terrible odds," his mate said.

"Mostly bruises," Kenny said, patting his side.

It had been worse than that. For a couple of days he'd thought he'd cracked a rib and had finally gone to A & E. He had massive bruising. Worse though was the pain when he went for a pee. The doctor thought he may have taken a blow to his kidneys and he'd had to take strong antibiotics for ten days. The scrape on his face had only just healed. He was looking better but still a little raw.

"I've forgotten your name," he said.

"Mack. People call me Mack. This here is Spenser. See, Mack and Spenser. Get it?"

Jimmy Mackintosh. That was his full name, Kenny remembered.

"I'm Kenny Harris. You look different," Kenny said, gesturing to the football shirt.

"I dress for the occasion. I don't wear casuals to work and I don't wear suits to football. We're just off for a bacon roll. Come and join us."

"I was just getting some cash," Kenny said.

"My treat, mate. You saved me a lot of bother bringing this back."

In the café Kenny and Mack sat at a table while Spenser went up to the counter.

"You live round here?" Mack said.

"Bow? St Peter's Square?"

"I know. There's a wine merchants there? My dad uses it."

47

"I live across the square from it!" Kenny said.

"Like football? Support a team?" Mack said, his shoulders squaring up again, showing off the full width of his away shirt.

"Not really. I watch it on telly sometimes."

Spenser arrived with a tray. On it were three mugs and three bacon rolls. He lifted each one off delicately, as if he were a waiter in a restaurant.

"Telly's rubbish. You've got to be there. To sniff the excitement. To hear the crowd. To feel the *danger*."

"Danger?" Kenny smiled, picking up his bacon roll.

"Drama, he means," said Spenser, sitting across from Kenny.

The two men started to talk about the coming game, including Kenny, as if he were a lifelong fan who knew everything about the team. Kenny looked at Spenser. He was thinner than Mack and older, maybe thirty or so. His head was almost bald, there was just the shadow of hair growth around the sides. He wasn't wearing a replica shirt but had on an expensive label shortsleeved shirt. On his forearm was a tattoo, *Mandy*. Spenser saw him looking at it.

"My daughter," he explained. "She's five!"

"How come you haven't got a West Ham shirt on?" Kenny said, after a while when both men had stopped talking and were eating their rolls.

"Tempting fate. This was how we went last Saturday. Mack in the away shirt, me in the Paul Smith. Team won. Can't change what we're wearing."

Kenny shook his head in amusement. Mack looked

up at him, his forehead in a momentary frown. Then he grinned.

"Boy thinks we're nuts!"

"But he won't say it!"

"Not nuts," Kenny said. "Just a bit *unbalanced*!"

"Boy's got a sense of humour, Spense."

"With a face like that he needs one!"

They both laughed. Kenny smiled good-humouredly. Then they went back to talking about West Ham. He stopped listening. He glanced at the time on his mobile. He should go. Then he remembered that Joe's girlfriend, Natalie, was coming round. Joe had said to him, *Nat likes you!* He pictured her face, small, elf-like, with fair hair that stuck up on top and flicked round her cheeks.

Joe was saving money, so Natalie was in the house a lot of the time. Kenny was finding it difficult to be around the pair of them. When he was at home he couldn't stay away from them, watching them together, registering Natalie's physical closeness to his brother. If she touched him with her hand it made Kenny feel unhappy. If she was playful with him it made Kenny want to get up and walk away. If he stumbled on them kissing it made his head swim and his body stiffen with desire and frustration. When he walked past Joe's closed bedroom door and heard Natalie speak low or laugh it made him inexplicably angry.

He wanted her.

It was better to stay out of the way. In a week or so Joe would be back at uni and Natalie wouldn't be a constant presence. He could forget about her.

It wasn't as if there weren't other girls. Kenny had never had any trouble with girls. He liked girls. He liked being mates with them; Tania, Penny, Michelle, Ruth, all girls from his class. He wasn't one of the boys who congregated in the common room and talked about how far they could get with girls. A hand on a breast or fingers sliding under a skirt or edging down some jeans. These things just weren't an interesting enough conversation for him. He was sick of boys telling their stories of what the girls in class had done for them. Sometimes he'd look at the girls in question and think of the stories that had been pushed down his ear, and he found it hard to imagine the events described taking place. Tania and her carefully painted nails, resting her hand on the crotch of some loudmouth boy's jeans. Michelle with her yellow hair hanging like a curtain, slipping her bra off in the back of a car. It just didn't seem feasible that these sweet-smelling girls would allow themselves to be handled by such desperate boys, who only seemed interested in their body parts.

Kenny *liked* being with girls, talking to them about their lives, their plans, the movies they liked, their essays. He just liked *talking* to them. He enjoyed it and never pushed it any further.

So, at first, it surprised him that the girls he was mates with often took matters into their own hands. More than once he had been pinned up against a wall with some chatty girl who had turned her words into wet frothy kisses before taking his hand and placing it firmly on her breast. He knew the sheer joy of unhooking a bra or unzipping jeans, his fingers only moving where they were welcome. It wasn't difficult, and it happened in a variety of ways as he got older, a couple of girls being prepared to go much further, pulling him into dark places that he had never been before. He never had any trouble getting off with girls. Not with Natalie, though. She was forbidden. It was better that he stayed away from her.

"You're miles away, young Ken," Spenser said, clicking his fingers in front of Kenny's face.

"Just thinking about the team's chances this season."

They both laughed and the three of them got up from the table. As they left the café Spenser patted Kenny on the shoulder.

"See this Paul Smith?" he said, pointing at his shirt, "I can get these knock-off, a quarter of the price. Let me know if you want one."

The three of them walked through the main shopping area. Kenny glanced around at the shops as Mack and Spenser peeled off in a different direction. He looked at the windows of Marks and Spencer's.

"I get it!" he shouted, pointing at the high street store. "Mack and Spenser! Very funny!"

Mack paused and shouted back, his voice loud, making shoppers look around.

"You should see a football match, young Kenny. Make a man out of you."

Then he walked off.

A week later Kenny came in from school and found an envelope on the floor in his hallway with his name on it. He opened it and found a ticket for a football match. The date was for the following Wednesday. A South London club. He turned it over and there, stuck to the back of it was a Post-it. In neat writing were the words

Come see the Hammers. Pick you up at five. Be ready. Mack.

EIGHT
SUNDAY, 18 DECEMBER, 2.14 A.M.

Jack's All-Nite Café was like a hothouse. Maurice was behind the counter as usual, looking serious, pen in hand, staring into his crossword book.

"Shut the door," he shouted without even glancing up.

Kenny pulled the door closed behind him, cutting off the freezing air that had followed him in. He pushed his hood back and pulled down the zip of his jacket. In the corner by the cigarette machine was the woman with the pink hair and crutches. She was sitting in her usual place. Two men were opposite. They were all playing cards. They looked up briefly and gave him a nod. There were half a dozen or so other people dotted around. A couple on their own staring into space. The rest in pairs, some eating, others sipping from Maurice's giant mugs. Kenny recognized a couple of them.

He walked up to the counter.

"Sausage sandwich and a coffee," he said.

"Politeness doesn't cost anything," Maurice said, taking a small pencil from behind his ear and writing on his book.

"Please, Maurice, and thank you?" Kenny said with a hint of exasperation in his voice.

"What's happened to you?" Maurice said, glancing up. He looked down at his crossword and finished filling in a word. Then he turned the corner of the page down and placed the book and the pencil carefully to one side. "Been in the wars?"

"Just a sausage sandwich and a mug of hot coffee, please?" Kenny said, giving a fake smile.

"No need for sarcasm, young Kenny. No need at all. You could do with some of your brother's ways," Maurice said. "How is young Joe?"

Kenny blew through his teeth. Maurice called anyone under forty *young*. Kenny answered in his politest voice.

"He's home for Christmas. I expect he'll be in any day."

"Have a seat. I'll bring the food over."

Kenny sat down near the window. Maybe something proper to eat would revive him. He might have a long wait for Tommy. That's if the man showed at all. Maybe he was tucked up in bed and Kenny would have to go to his flat. That was something he didn't want to do. The CCTV cameras around the estate would pick him up, he was sure. He looked at his old mobile. The time numerals on the screen were bigger and bolder than on his new one: 02:22. It was disconcerting. It was as if the number had grown larger to remind him that his time was running out. He looked away, pushing the mobile into his pocket.

Tommy hadn't been in any of the pubs in Walthamstow that Mack had suggested. Nor had he been in the gym at Leyton. Kenny had waited until it closed and the last person had left. If Tommy was out at a party, or a late-night boozer, then he would drop into the café at some time. That was almost certain. How many times had Kenny been in the café on a Saturday night and seen Tommy Fortune slope in, looking red-faced, his bow tie askew. If not Tommy, then maybe some of his mates would come. Then he really could listen to their conversations and find out where Tommy was.

He looked out through the window. Even though it was the middle of the night there was still activity outside the café. The minicab place next door was still open and there were a couple of cars parked close by, their interior lights on, showing the drivers reading or talking into their radios. Every now and then the windscreen wipers flicked across, clearing the glass of sleet. One of the drivers lifted a cigarette to his lips and lit it with a match. It made Kenny feel like a smoke. If ever he needed some calm time it was now.

He looked around the café. The woman with pink hair had just won a hand and was laughing and coughing at the same time. One of her companions was stretching his arms up to the ceiling, letting a couple of cards flutter down from his fingers. The other one was round-shouldered, patting in his back pocket for something. He had a cigarette sticking out of his mouth, unlit.

55

The woman with the pink hair was always in the café, always in that seat, often playing cards or backgammon, or occasionally chess. She'd been there the first ever night that Kenny had come in. In the summer, it was. His brother Joe had been home from uni and had taken him there after a party. They'd lingered for a long time over mugs of tea and Kenny had found himself staring at the pink hair and the crutches and wondering what the woman's story was. She'd looked as though she was holding a fan in front of her face. At a second glance it turned out to be a hand of cards. He'd been to the café maybe twenty times since and she'd always been there. A fixture.

After that first night he'd visited the café a lot. He and Joe had been there together a few times. Actually they'd been getting on quite well in those weeks before Joe met Natalie. Joe's first year at uni meant that he was absent from the house and Kenny had actually *got on* with him when he came home during the holidays. He hadn't even minded Joe going on about politics and the rights of the workers. He and Russell and Joe had gone out together, often after the Scarlet Lady had shut, and had ended up in the café. Tommy Fortune was usually around, especially in the early hours of Sunday morning. It was as if a visit to the café was obligatory to go over the events of Saturday night.

"Sausage sandwich. Coffee. Three pound and five pence, call it three pound."

Maurice's voice broke into Kenny's thoughts. He gave Maurice a weak smile and handed him the money.

Kenny bit into his sandwich. He first got talking to Tommy Fortune because of the DVDs. Tommy had a zip-up bag bursting with sets of *The Sopranos*. *Ten quid each one*, Tommy had said. Ten pounds for a whole series. He'd bought two that night and pleaded with Tommy to hold back the others until he had the money. Tommy had pulled on his tie and straightened his collar. *You haven't got the money. Story of my life! Still, you're Joe's brother. You can owe me the money. Here's my card!* he'd said and produced a handful of small printed cards, *Tommy Fortune, Businessman*. Underneath was an email address and a mobile number.

Kenny had given him the money and Tommy always sought him out when he had new crime DVDs. *They're surplus stock*, he said but everyone knew that they were nicked. Occasionally Joe bought some dope from Tommy which he passed on to Kenny and Russell.

Now Kenny had to find Tommy and sell something to him. He had to persuade him to go with him to the Sugar House. The thought of it made him feel full up suddenly and he lowered his half-eaten sandwich. How badly would Mack have to hurt Tommy Fortune in order to *put the frighteners on him*?

He thought of the letter in his back pocket. Using his good hand he pulled it out and unfolded the envelope. It wasn't a thick wad of paper, just one side of A4 tucked inside an envelope. He'd never been much for writing stories or notes or even essays. On the outside he'd written a name, DI Parsons, followed by the address of the police station at Epping. He'd even put a first class stamp on it.

Would he ever post it?

Just then a figure shot past the window and came into the café, opening and closing the door so quickly that Kenny would have sworn it hadn't moved.

"Brass monkeys out there!"

It was Johnson, one of Tommy's mates. He was rubbing his hands together, hugging himself and moving from foot to foot to warm up. Kenny sat up, pushed the letter back into his jeans pocket. He picked up his sandwich, even though he'd decided not to eat any more.

"Thought of wearing a coat?" Maurice shouted, dryly.

"Just come from London Hospital," Johnson said, as though someone had asked him where he'd been. "Tommy's been beaten up!"

Without turning round, without looking bothered, Kenny listened.

"There was a lock-in at the Feathers and he was dancing a little too lively, if you know what I mean. Somebody got the needle," Johnson said, moving towards Maurice and away from Kenny.

"Is it bad?"

Kenny could hear Maurice asking the question but he didn't hear the reply. He had already opened the door and slipped out of the warm café. He stood still for a moment to pull his hood up, the sleet hitting his skin like tiny pebbles. Then he headed off up the street towards the London Hospital.

NINE
NATALIE

Natalie woke with a start and looked round at the dark room. Something had beeped. A second later it beeped again, a familiar sound. She sat up, reached across and turned on the bedside light. Kenny's mobile lit up suddenly and beeped for a third time. She tutted. She should have turned it off before she went to sleep.

There was a message. In the middle of the night? Surely Kenny was in bed, asleep. Why would someone send him messages at that time of night? She pushed the *silent* button and lay back on her pillow. The room was cold so she pulled the duvet up to her neck. She closed her eyes but opened them again almost immediately. She was wide awake. She looked at her clock. There were hours to go until morning.

It was becoming a regular thing, not being able to sleep. Kenny's recent mood had been troubling her, *depressing* her. When he finally came back to see her, days after his birthday, she'd been thrilled. They'd lain on the bed, Kenny staring up at the ceiling and she kissing and touching him. She'd lain on top of him and he'd responded. He'd held her tightly, his breaths puffing out between kisses, his hands skirting around her, making her pant with passion. But then he'd pulled back, kept his clothes on, made some joke about her wearing him out. In moments he was gone, the back door banging as he crept out through her garden and away into the night.

Getting up to change into her nightclothes she'd found the unused condom sachet on the floor by the bed. She'd picked it up and put in a drawer, tucking it far away at the back.

The next couple of nights it was the same. She hadn't been able to work out what was going on. It was as though he wasn't really there in the room with her. He hardly answered when she spoke, and when he did he had a kind of delayed reaction as though her words were in a queue in his brain.

The previous night she'd asked him outright, *Do you want to finish?* She was prepared for it. If he didn't want her then she'd walk away. *Do you want us to finish?* she'd said, holding his face so that he had to look straight at her and take notice of what she was saying.

He'd shaken his head and pulled her into his chest so that she could hardly breathe. He'd edged her on to the bed and unbuttoned her shirt, pulling each sleeve off carefully, slipping her skirt off, letting it drop on to the floor, until her white lacy pants and bra were all she had on. She'd reached for him, her eyes closing, her lips dry, her heart racing.

But then he sat up, his elbows on his knees, his face in his hands. After a while he went home. Was he still thinking about Joe? Natalie didn't know. She was afraid to ask him. Even though she had been Joe's girlfriend she had got off lightly. It was ten times worse for him than it had been for her.

Natalie sat up, disgruntled. She pulled the duvet back. As she wasn't going to sleep she might as well do something. She pulled on some tracksuit bottoms, a fleecy top and some slippers. She went downstairs and made herself a cup of tea. Blowing the steam off the top she went back up into her room and sat on the bed. The blue letter on the carpet immediately caught her eye.

She picked it up. Joe's letter. It must have dropped from her fingers earlier. She took it over to her drawer to put it with the others. How typical of Joe to write her letters when he could have sent emails. It was more *romantic*, he'd said. She hesitated. Why did she keep them? What for? She pulled them out and carried them back to the bed. There were nine or ten. Once back at uni he'd sent one every few days. All the news of the course, his essays, his discussions, his thoughts. *I miss you*, he'd said. *Hope you're not missing me too much!* Just thinking of the words brought back that heavy feeling in her chest. Guilt. She hadn't missed him. Not at all.

She'd first met Joe at the pub round the corner, the Scarlet Lady. It was in June, the last day of her exams. She and a couple of friends went there at lunch time for a celebratory drink and had ended up staying all afternoon. He was working behind the bar. He was good-looking in a hippie sort of way, his hair long, a strand of wooden beads around his neck. He had chatted to her as he served her with drinks. She told him why she was there and he said he'd just finished his first year at uni. She'd asked him all about it until his boss had shouted at him and told him to collect glasses from the tables outside.

Later in the afternoon, after too many drinks, she'd ended up sitting on a wall outside with her head on her knees. He'd come over, been concerned, found her friend and made sure she got a cab home. She told him her address so that he could tell the driver. The next day she saw him waiting outside her house in his car.

That was how it started. For weeks they spent a lot of time together. He was different to the other lads she knew. He was idealistic, interested in things that were going on in other countries. He was involved in various groups which campaigned for stuff; workers' rights in South America, ending Third World debt, Fair Trade in coffee and bananas. He was even writing letters to a prisoner on Death Row in Atlanta.

She'd never met anyone like him before. It all seemed very *grown up*. He was passionate when he talked about these things and was keen to know her views. When they did stop talking and start to hold each other he was slow and easy. He didn't rush things. They kissed and touched and lay together, but there was no sex. *We've got loads of time for that*, he'd said, rolling away from her, picking up a book or newspaper to read.

She liked it. It meant that she was humming with desire most of the time. A few kisses with him made her stomach squirm and her skin tickle. He was in no rush. It made her feel mature.

One weekend he took her home to meet his family. His mum and dad were in the living room and she shook hands with each of them and talked about her courses at college and they seemed interested. *They loved you!* Joe whispered as he led her out and towards the kitchen. He pushed the door open and she was faced with Kenny.

"Meet my girlfriend," he said, and then turning to her, "This is Kenny, my little brother."

Kenny wasn't little, though. He was as big as Joe and fuller. His hair was dark and short and his face tanned. He had jeans on and a shirt that he hadn't buttoned up yet. He stepped forward and put his hand out to shake hers. His grip was strong.

"Hello," she said.

"I hope you're looking after my big brother?" he said. "He does nothing but talk about you!"

She blushed and found herself looking straight at him. He caught her eye and held her look for a few seconds. Then Joe walked between them breaking the contact.

Was it love at first sight? She would have laughed if anyone had said that. He was just a boy, just a school-boy.

When they left the house later Joe paused for a moment on the path and kissed her hard on the mouth.

63

It took her by surprise and her eyes stayed open. She found herself looking over his shoulder. There, at the living room window, behind the net curtain, was Kenny, looking straight at them.

She raised her hand in a tiny wave. It was a beginning.

Natalie gathered the letters up off her duvet. Maybe she should throw them away. Kenny might not like it if he found them.

She glanced over at his mobile. Although it was quiet there was a glow coming from it. Another message. She picked it up and pressed the keys. There were two messages. She listened. The first was from Jimmy Mackintosh.

Kenny, mate, you need to get back to me. If you let me down I'll come looking for you. I want this sorted out by morning. I mean it, Kenny. Don't chicken out on me, you've got as much to lose as I have. Ring me.

Natalie frowned. The second one, received about fifteen minutes later, came on. It was also from Jimmy Mackintosh. The voice was the same but there was a different sound to it. It was lower, husky. Some of the words sounded cracked.

Kenny, I lost my temper earlier. I shouldn't have hit you. I know that. I just see red sometimes and I can't help it. But I don't want no trouble from you, Kenny. Me and you, we're mates. I'm depending on you.

It was Jimmy Mackintosh who had hit Kenny, had beaten him up. She frowned. What was wrong with that man? She pressed the button and listened again. She checked the time of the last message. Just ten minutes before. He was expecting Kenny to do something but she had his mobile. Maybe it was important. She stood up as if she was about to go somewhere. She stepped across to the window. It was pitch dark, the Christmas lights on the tree had switched off. Snow was hitting the glass but it didn't look as though it was settling anywhere. She couldn't go out. She needed to get in touch with Kenny but how could she? She couldn't ring his house, his mother wouldn't speak to her and in any case it was the middle of the night. She accessed Kenny's contacts and scrolled down until she came to *Jimmy Mack*. What if she rang him? To say that she had Kenny's mobile.

A feeling of distaste made her hesitate. Then she saw, just below, on Kenny's list of contacts, was the name *Joe*.

Joe's letter said he was coming home early. Maybe he was already there. She could text him. He could wake up Kenny. He'd do that, wouldn't he? He wouldn't hold a grudge against his own brother when it might be something important? If he was asleep and didn't get the message, well, she'd done what she could.

She sat on the bed and began her text message.

Dear Joe, Natalie here, Kenny left his mobile at my house and I need to get in touch with him asap. I think he might be in some sort of trouble. Can you wake him?

She pressed *send* and sat back on the bed.

TEN

SUNDAY, 18 DECEMBER, 2.51 A.M.

Accident and Emergency was quiet. There was only the distant sound of cartoon voices from a television screen. A security guard was standing with his back against a wall, looking up at it. There were Christmas decorations draped around and a sign that said, *London Hospital wishes all patients and carers a Happy Christmas*. Underneath there were translations in other languages.

A black woman was on reception. She was reading a thick paperback book. A nurse was walking sedately towards some doors carrying a mug. One man was lying across three chairs fast asleep. At the other end a woman and an older woman were sitting tightly together. That was it. No Tommy Fortune.

A nurse appeared and walked smartly up to him.

"You have to check in at reception. Then take a seat. It shouldn't be long and we'll get you looked at."

He gave Kenny a nudge towards the counter. Kenny

66

looked at his hand, the bandages were a little battered and feeling wet. They thought he was here for treatment. Maybe that wasn't such a bad thing. He took a deep breath and went up to reception.

"Excuse me," he said, in a whisper, "the nurse said to come here?"

The woman looked up from her book and gave a thin smile. Her hair was plaited and she had flat red earrings that looked like Smarties. She put her book to one side and picked up a pen.

"Name?" she said.

Kenny answered. There was nothing odd about him being in Casualty. He was injured. Everyone he'd seen tonight knew that. It gave him an excuse to be there. That way he could look for Tommy.

There were more questions and he answered them as quickly as he could. Then he was directed to the seats. He sat close to the treatment area and watched every time the double doors burst open. If Tommy was here he was through those doors. Beside him was a table with magazines strewn across it. He ignored them and watched the doors.

He waited. No one came out. No one went in. No one moved in the waiting area. It was as if time was standing still. Only the images on the TV changed. He looked around, his eye settling on tiny CCTV cameras on the walls of the waiting area. He counted them. There were six, spaced out, all pointing in different directions. Kenny imagined a security man in a room looking at a line of screens, all showing different parts of the

67

hospital. If Tommy was there he didn't want to be seen with him.

He stood up to stretch his legs. A dull ache was returning to his injured thigh. Maybe the paracetamol was wearing off. He sat down again. The bandage on his hand felt loose, his fingers able to move. Maybe he should have his injuries looked at. Possibly he was in worse shape than he thought. They might give him a painkilling injection and he would sleep the night away. Then he wouldn't be *able* to get hold of Tommy.

The double doors opened and Tommy Fortune suddenly came out. The sight of him startled Kenny, and he froze for a moment. A nurse was holding Tommy by the elbow and pointing at a door over the far side of A & E.

The man was a mess, the flesh around his eye was swollen and his forehead was grazed. One of his arms was in a sling. He was wearing his customary suit but he had no dicky bow on and it didn't look as if he was wearing a coat. He looked rough.

Kenny stopped staring. He picked up a magazine and held it up in front of his face. Out the corner of his eye he saw Tommy nod to the nurse and walk towards the far door. There was a sign that said *Island Cafeteria*. He waited, hardly breathing, letting Tommy walk away. When the doors closed behind him Kenny counted to twenty slowly in his head, put the magazine down and got up.

"I can see you now," a voice said.

The male nurse was standing next to him, a pleasant look on his face.

"No, it's OK, I'm all right . . . I've changed my mind," Kenny said, sidestepping him and walking in the direction of the doors.

He heard grumbling noises from behind but he ignored them and went through the doors and followed the signs to the Island Cafeteria.

The cafeteria was steamy. It was a small space, ten or twelve tables stretching towards some doors marked EXIT TO STREET. Two hospital workers were sitting at one table, eating heartily, knives and forks scraping at their plates. Tommy Fortune was sitting in a seating area holding the receiver of a wall phone. Above the telephone Kenny saw a sign that said *Minicabs Freefone*.

Kenny hesitated. Tommy would probably leave by that exit and pick up the cab outside. He needed to go out there and wait in the street so that when Tommy left the cafeteria it would look as though he'd just run in to him.

But where would Tommy go in the cab? Home?

Kenny's heart sank. He would have to go in the cab with him. It meant that someone would see him with Tommy and that was exactly what Mack said he shouldn't do. But what choice did he have? He would have to pull his hood up, avoid looking straight at the driver, not speak.

Whatever. He had to keep with Tommy.

Tommy had replaced the receiver and was walking towards the food counter. Maybe he was getting a drink. Possibly the cab had said it would be a while. Kenny made an instant decision. He stepped into the cafeteria and without looking left or right he made for the exit. In less than twenty seconds he was across the room.

He went through the doors and found himself in the street at the side of the hospital. The darkness was heavy and the cold air nibbled his ears. On the ground he could see dog-ends scattered like confetti. He felt his breaths jagging in his chest. With his good hand he got his inhaler out. It was really too soon to use it again, but he needed it.

In a short while he would be with Tommy Fortune, the person he had been looking for for hours. He moved his weight from one foot to the other as a feeling of unease wafted through him. He leaned against the wall. He thought about Mack. He imagined him sitting down somewhere waiting for Kenny to arrive. Where? In some dark corner of the Sugar House? Or in his car? What would he do while he was waiting? Listen to music? The radio? Think about what he was going to do to Tommy? Kenny felt panic rising in his throat.

He had to pull himself together.

It might not be as bad as he thought. Just because Mack had said some hard things, had made some threats; it didn't mean he would necessarily carry them out. It might just be enough for Mack to explain to Tommy what he intended to do. Tommy wasn't an idiot.

Tommy might refuse to go with him. He'd just been beaten up, maybe the nurses had given him some painkillers. Most likely he wanted to go home and sleep it off. It wasn't as if he could kidnap Tommy. Mack would have to understand. Kenny couldn't work miracles. On the other hand Tommy might just come. If Kenny spun him a story about someone selling knocked-off iPods Tommy would probably walk through fire to get them.

And then what? Once Tommy arrived he might face an awful beating and it would be he, Kenny, who had delivered him. He thought of Tommy's face, already bruised by some punch-up in a pub. How could Mack hit him again? A feeling of hopelessness settled on Kenny and he pressed his face up against the brick wall of the hospital.

"Are you all right, son?"

A voice broke into his thoughts. Startled he looked around. It was a WPC. A hefty woman squeezed into the uniform, a half-smile on her face.

"Are you feeling all right?" she said, her smile fading, her eyebrows crinkling.

Kenny looked at her with dismay. A policewoman. She mustn't see him anywhere near Tommy.

"I was just looking for Casualty," he said, raising his bandaged hand.

"That's round the front of the hospital. Just go to the corner and turn right," she said, pointing towards the high street.

"Thanks," Kenny said, heading off, shivering suddenly as if his body had only just registered the cold.

What now?

He turned right and then stopped. He bent down as if to do up a shoelace. Then walking slowly back he peeped back round the corner. The WPC was still there. He swore, pulled his mobile out and looked at the time. The big numerals stared back at him, 03:20. They seemed to take up all of the screen. He shoved it back in his pocket as a saloon car came along and turned down the street towards the cafeteria exit. The cab. Kenny swallowed. He looked round the corner again. The WPC was gone and Tommy Fortune stood in the doorway as the cab approached.

He headed round the corner. The cab stopped, its handbrake making a sharp moan. Tommy took a step to the cab and Kenny shouted his name. He looked round, a little shaky, the white of his sling standing out against the dark.

"I thought it was you," Kenny said, and then lowering his voice he added, "It's me, Kenny Harris? Joe's brother?"

Tommy gave a tired smile. Kenny looked at the doors of the hospital. There was no sign of the WPC.

"I've been looking for you. I've got a deal you might be interested in. Some iPods. You were the first person I thought of. Why don't I come back to your place for a cup of tea and we can talk about it?"

Tommy Fortune looked amused, or dazed. Kenny wasn't quite sure which.

The cab driver tooted his horn lightly. Kenny opened the door.

"You get in first, Tommy," he said, pulling the

drawstring on his hood so that the driver could only see a small oval of his face.

Tommy mumbled something, got in and Kenny followed.

ELEVEN
FOOTBALL MACK-STYLE

Kenny could hardly breathe. All around him the fans were standing on seats, screaming, singing, shouting, pointing and making deep throaty sounds. He felt like he was an onlooker in a battle. Mack glanced at him a couple of times and nodded his head, looking pleased with himself. It was as if he *wanted* to see Kenny looking out of place.

Mack and Spenser were wearing the exact same clothes that they'd been wearing on the Saturday he'd found Mack's cashcard.

"What do you think of the team?" Mack shouted into his ear.

Kenny nodded approvingly.

"No, no. They're rubbish!" Mack shouted.

Kenny was puzzled. Mack had picked him up at his house and driven halfway across London. They'd had to park miles away from the ground and walk through throngs of people. The beer was expensive and anyway they didn't have time to finish their pints before going into the stands. The seats were tiny, the place heaving with fans. Even though it was an October evening he could feel the heat from the crowd. He could see the pitch but had to keep sitting down and standing up whenever the crowd did. When he looked in one direction he was dazzled by the giant flood-lights.

Mack had spent a lot of money on this ticket, yet it was much more comfortable to watch it on TV. Kenny didn't say this though. He sensed that it would be the wrong attitude. Real football fans enjoyed the agony as much as the joy. Kenny just wasn't a *real* football fan. He looked from side to side at Mack and Spenser. They were glued to the action, their heads rotating whenever the ball went down one end or the other. They were tense, their backs and arms rigid, their mouths held in a sneer. Ready to slag off the opposing team, or their own if they felt like it.

The full-time score was nil–nil.

They sat on the seats while other fans moved along the rows and made their way out of the ground. There was no point in rushing, Mack had said, they might as well wait until it was less crowded. He winked at Spenser and Spenser eyed Kenny, with some delight. It was as if they both had a secret that they were keeping between themselves, passing it back and forth, waiting for Kenny to tackle one or other of them.

"Remember that kid from the tube station. The one who was giving you a kicking?" Mack said.

"Tibbs?" Kenny said.

Kenny wouldn't forget Jon Tibbs with his round glasses. The humiliation of being beaten up. Three against one. In front of Natalie.

"I see him the other day. He was taking this dog for a walk. Me and Spenser were sitting outside a pub. I said to Spenser, he's got it coming to him."

"Tell him about the dog," Spenser said, smiling.

"One of those little yappy terriers. Old, waddling. The lad had to keep stopping and coaxing him on. I reckon he was doing a job for his mum."

Kenny didn't want to think of Jon Tibbs walking a dog. He didn't want to think about him at all. He let his mind drift off as Mack and Spenser started talking about dogs. He thought about the long car journey through London and the things Spenser had told Kenny about Mack and himself.

Mack was twenty-five. He worked in an insurance company. *Good job. Computer security! Spends all his day on the Internet looking at porn sites*, Spenser had said. Mack had disagreed from the driver's seat. When he told him how much he earned Kenny was impressed. The car should have given it away. A BMW that was only a year or so old. *Still lives with his mum and dad though!* Spenser said.

Spenser was married and had a five-year-old daughter called Mandy. He worked as an electrician in Stansted Airport. *Cheap flights!* he said. *And plenty of other stuff.*

By the time they'd arrived at the South London

ground Kenny knew that Mack's mum and dad spent most of the winter in Tenerife while he looked after their house. Spencer's wife wanted another baby but Spenser wasn't sure. Mack and Spenser had been to school together. Mack was the one with the brains. Spenser had credit-card debts. Mack had money in the bank.

The two friends were still talking about which dog they'd like to buy.

"A boxer, definitely," Mack said. "A man's dog."

"Boxers are good," Spenser said. "But I like the springers."

"Springers are brilliant hunting dogs."

"And we like to hunt," Spenser said.

"You hunt?" Kenny said, looking round the stadium, realizing that most of the people had gone. "Rabbits?"

"Nah, we like to hunt people. . ." Mack said, giving a sideways look at Spenser.

Kenny didn't comment. He took a few steps in the direction of the exit. He had a feeling that he was having the mickey taken out of him. He was fed up. Football wasn't really his game. He'd only come because Mack had paid for his ticket. Also it suited him to get out of the house. It was Joe's last night at home and Nat was staying overnight. Kenny was surprised that his mum and dad had allowed it, but then it was *Joe* who had asked.

He'd left Natalie and Joe cooking pasta in the kitchen. The scene had annoyed him, Natalie's bare arms brushing against his brother's shirtsleeves. Her midriff showing every time she reached up for something. His brother hugging her just because she'd chopped up the onions properly.

If she was his he'd just take her upstairs and keep her in his room. He'd draw the curtains and put the chair against his door. He'd wrap her up in his bedclothes and kiss her mouth until she was dizzy. Never mind about chopping up onions.

No doubt his mum and dad allowed the sleepover because they thought Joe would be sensible. Joe had probably downloaded all the relevant information on *contraception* from the Internet. The thought of it filled Kenny with derision. He could smile and mock his brother but there was also jealousy snaking around inside him.

He had to stay out of the house.

Mack and Spenser were some way behind him and Kenny turned to see that they were talking to four other fans who had appeared as if from nowhere in the near empty ground. They were talking and laughing and shoving each other playfully. They eyed Kenny and Mack said something about him. Then they all walked in his direction.

"Something's come up. We've got some business with some of the opposing team," Mack said, as he reached Kenny.

"Trouble?" Kenny said.

"Depends on your point of view. Come along and see. You don't have to join in!"

The other fans laughed. They were all in their

twenties, looking like different versions of Mack and Spenser. Kenny looked around the stadium. How could there be trouble? There was no one left.

"It's been prearranged," Mack said. "The World Wide Web. It's a wonderful thing," he added, passing Kenny and heading purposefully towards the exit, the others following close.

"This is something we do, young Ken. It's set up on the Internet. No one gets hurt. Not *really* hurt. It's a battle, see. They've *challenged* us. We're like *warriors*."

Warriors. Kenny almost laughed out loud. But Spenser walked off and Kenny followed slowly as they exited the ground. Outside the police were standing around and there were a couple of nearby vans with officers sitting waiting. He looked at his watch. He didn't want to get involved in trouble. He hesitated. Getting public transport home would be a pain. He might as well stay with Mack and Spenser and the others. The fight would probably come to nothing.

As they walked on Mack hung back and put his arm around Kenny's shoulders. He felt momentarily awkward. If any of his mates had done it he would have felt bad, embarrassed. None of them would. But Mack was different. He did it firmly as if it was the most natural thing in the world. He spoke quietly to Kenny.

"We meet them at a prearranged place. It's us against them, see. You absolutely don't get involved. Just hang back. I'll make sure no one touches you."

Kenny found himself strutting. Was Mack saying he

wasn't *allowed* to get involved? Mack seemed to sense the change in him.

"There are rules, right. Younger brothers, mates, don't get involved. It's like against like. You get involved and it looks bad on us."

They'd walked a fair way from the ground and without warning the other fans turned left, down an alley, and the rest followed. Kenny instantly felt apprehensive. Mack strode up ahead, leaving Kenny with Spenser.

"There's an old disused loading bay back here. Used to be a bakery. Closed a while back. We've been here before. Last season."

The alley was dark but there was a light up ahead. A gate was hanging open. He could see the faded lettering. *Winterbottom's Quality Breads and Cakes Estab. 1949.* He followed the others inside. He found himself in a square courtyard, a few crates dotted around and a single rusting forklift truck washed up in a corner. On the ground, in the middle, was a heavy lamp, the kind used on building sites. Some men emerged from the darkness and Kenny felt a prickle of fear at the back of his neck. A boy walked through the courtyard, picked up the lamp, headed for the forklift truck and sat on it. He was twelve or thirteen. The men stood across from them, their faces hard. Mack nudged him and pointed at the concrete loading bay. Kenny walked over and sat on it, his insides churning.

He wished he hadn't come. He didn't avoid fights. He'd been in some over the years. But he didn't seek them out and anyhow this wasn't a fight as he knew it. When feelings were hurt or insults were thrown, when he felt slighted or embarrassed or even humiliated: those were the moments to have a fight. Sometimes there was nothing else that would do except to strike out, using a fist or a foot or a head.

This was different. Like extras on a film set the men – six on one side, six on the other – stood waiting; as if for a signal, a starting pistol, a man with a clapperboard saying *Action*.

Mack started it. He walked up to the man opposite him and pushed him backwards. That was it. The signal. There was noise and rushing and suddenly the men were in a heap, punching, kicking, shouting. One dragging another by the arm to a place where he could sit astride him and pummel away at his cheeks, one fist neatly after the other like someone boxing a punchbag.

Kenny froze for three or four minutes, just watching, hardly breathing as the men kicked and swore, their arms gripping on to their opponents, using their heads to ram this way and that. Then he felt his body moving as if to join in, to defend his new mates, but the ferocity of the scene held him back. Two men were pulling someone by the arms and legs, another man was being held in an armlock, dragged backwards, kicking his legs out. Kenny looked up for a moment and saw the twelve year old, across the way, lit up in a beam of light, using his fists, gesticulating, excitement written all over his face.

Then it stopped.

The whine of a siren in the distance seemed to be a signal, and the men disengaged and retreated. Left in the centre of the courtyard was a man in a foetal position, his hands cradling his ears. Standing above him was Mack, his knee raised as if stamp on the man. He hesitated for a moment and then lowered his leg and stepped back.

"Out!" he shouted.

They had to get away, in case the police siren had been for them. Mack and the others ran in one direction, Spenser in another, pulling Kenny by the elbow. Kenny followed him, deep into the old warehouse, and waited in the dark, breathing lightly. After about five minutes, when no one came, it was time to go. On their way through the courtyard they saw three of the opposing side tending to the man on the ground.

"Should we do something?" Kenny whispered, as they passed along the edge of the courtyard.

"Quick," Spenser said, running through.

"Do you think that man'll be all right?" Kenny said, puffing, heading for the bright lights of the street.

Spenser slowed down, shrugging his shoulders.

"I thought you said it wasn't going to be bad. I didn't think that Mack would be so intense. He made it sound like it was just a bit of—"

"I told you. It was a battle," Spenser said, walking rapidly.

"But that bloke. He's hurt. . ."

"Mack's done much worse than that. He's got a reputation."

"What's he done?" Kenny said.

"He killed a man."

"What?" Kenny said, his mouth open in disbelief.

"Mack killed a man. Two years ago," Spenser said. "I know because I was there when he did it."

TWELVE

Kenny was cross-legged on the floor while Tommy Fortune sat on an old battered settee. The TV was on showing the twenty-four-hour news channel, the volume low. Tommy had looked like he wanted to go off to bed but Kenny kept him talking. He told the story about the man he knew who had stolen iPods. It was a sure thing, he said, the man wanted to get rid of them quick and would meet Tommy at a place on West India Quays.

Tommy didn't look as though he was paying much attention but he was hospitable enough to nod his head and smile a lot. His face looked awful, purple and misshapen and he was holding the sling that was on his arm. Kenny wondered if his own face was that bad.

Tommy's flat was on the third floor of a low-rise block. Walking from the cab to the building Kenny had lagged behind Tommy and kept his head down in case of CCTV cameras. It didn't look like there were any though and the pair of them walked up three flights of stairs to get to the right floor. Tommy didn't like lifts. *Claustrophobia*, he explained.

The flats were neat and clean on the outside. Once inside Tommy's, it was a different matter. There was a heavy smell of something, and the hallway was stacked with boxes and piles of newspapers. It was hot, as if the heating was turned up to its highest setting. The living room was untidy and Tommy had to move clothes to make a space to sit down. Kenny didn't bother. He sat on the floor between a pile of magazines and an empty wastepaper bin. He glanced at the magazines. *World War Two, A Complete History*. There must have been twenty or more.

After he'd told the story of the iPods there was a few moments' quiet.

"I'll just lie down," Tommy said suddenly, pulling at the laces of his shoes with his free hand.

Kenny watched as Tommy kicked his shoes off and got himself comfortable. His eyes were open for a few moments but then they drooped and eventually closed and it wasn't long before Tommy was snoring gently, his lips apart, his bad arm dipping on to the settee. Kenny looked at Tommy's feet. He had red socks on. They stood out in the otherwise shabby room.

It was almost a relief that Tommy was sleeping. Now Kenny didn't have to keep up a story, to act positive and try and persuade Tommy to come. He was where he wanted to be, with Tommy, and there was still time before he had to meet Mack. He looked at his mobile.

He still had over two hours. A lot could happen. He could talk to Mack, get him to treat Tommy lightly, to *imply* violence rather than use it.

A sound from the sofa startled him. Tommy was turning over, struggling with his bandaged arm. It looked like he might wake up. It was almost as if Tommy knew what he was thinking, as if Kenny's thoughts about Tommy's fate had disturbed his sleep. He watched as the man settled again, his red socks making him look comic. It made Kenny feel desperately sad all of a sudden. There were no laughs to be had at Tommy's expense, none at all.

Mack could be reasonable. Most of the time he was. Only in extreme circumstances did he become dangerous. Like that night at the football, or earlier that evening when he beat Kenny up.

He closed his eyes, the sound of the TV news far in the background. The seventh of December. What a night that had been. *Got a great idea for your birthday present*, Mack had said. Kenny could hear his words, almost see his excited face.

For a moment Kenny thought that he was going to cry. He swallowed two, three times. He put his fingers over his eyelids to keep them shut tight. To stop the tears. To shut out the memory of Mack, grinning, *Come on, Kenny, this is my present for you. . .*

He patted his back pocket. The letter was still there. He'd written it all down and folded it away so that the story was there on paper rather than in his head.

In the dark of Epping Forest Mack had not been

reasonable. He'd been wild, out of control and it had ended in death.

Why should Kenny have been surprised?

It wasn't the first time Mack had killed a man.

THIRTEEN
WHEN MACK KILLED A MAN

After the football match and the fight Kenny suggested Jack's All-Nite Café. The three of them sat down at a table next to the window and cradled cups of hot chocolate. Behind them, in the corner, was the woman with the pink hair and crutches. Long stretches of quiet suggested a game of chess was going on. Out in the street the minicab office was busy, hazard lights winking on cars that were double parked, waiting for fares.

Kenny had been quiet in the car all the way from South London. He'd listened as the older men talked about the match and the fight and then, oddly, about someone they knew who was buying a house and which mortgage they used. Spenser described his attempts to buy a house, which Mack laughed at. *It's all right for you, you're still living at your mum and dad's!* Spenser had said.

How could they talk about such ordinary, mundane things? After the raw violence of the fight? Was it just an everyday event for them?

Pushing his empty mug away, Mack spoke quietly. "I'll have to chuck these jeans. Look at that. Ripped!"

Spenser mumbled a reply but Kenny couldn't hear it, didn't want to hear it. He looked at his watch. It wasn't even midnight. He didn't want to go home yet. Natalie and Joe were probably packing Joe's boxes, folding his clothes, sorting out his books. Or else they had left it all to one side and were rocking back and forward on Joe's bed. The thought of this made his stomach drop and he lowered his cup, unable to drink any of the sludgy liquid.

A beep sounded. Mack stood up and patted his pockets. He pulled his mobile out and looked at the screen. His face dropped.

"It's Kerry," he said, and flipped it open. "I'll have to do this in private."

He walked towards the door, talking as he went. Spenser made a face. When Mack was outside Spenser explained, "His girlfriend."

Kenny watched as Mack walked up and down the pavement, looking down at his clothes, or at the ground. He was talking animatedly, even smiling. Spenser was describing his wife's new mobile, which he had got when he changed tariffs. A freebie, he said, and then explained about the new tariff he'd agreed to.

Kenny focused on Mack outside, listening to his girlfriend. Across the table Spenser was talking about direct debits. It was bizarre to be sitting in a café drinking hot chocolate with these two everyday regular men, with jobs and families and bank accounts. Only a couple of hours before they'd been beating the hell out of strangers for no other reason than they'd arranged it on the Internet. Kenny didn't get it.

"Who did Mack kill?" he said suddenly, breaking into Spenser's monologue about bank charges.

Spenser looked puzzled as if he'd forgotten that he'd told Kenny. Then his face clouded.

"Don't ask," he said, in a half-whisper.

"What happened?" Kenny said. "I won't say anything to Mack."

"I can't talk about it. Mack doesn't talk about it now."

Spenser rubbed at his tattoo. Kenny was peeved. How could Spenser say something like that and not back it up?

"I'll ask Mack," he said, nonchalantly.

"No. Mack never talks about it. It's like dead and buried," Spencer said, and then grimaced. "Excuse the pun."

"Come on, mate. I'll never say a word. Not a word."

Spenser glanced out of the window. Mack was walking up and down pointing in mid-air as if in the middle of a quarrel. Spenser spoke quietly so that Kenny had to lean forward to listen.

"Two years ago. Mack and me were getting a pint in a pub off Oxford Street. It was about three in the afternoon. Some bloke knocks into Mack and spills his pint over Mack's new suit."

Spenser stopped.

"A Paul Smith it was," he said, sighing.

Kenny waited. A sound from behind made him turn

round. The woman with pink hair was clapping her hands, the game of chess finished.

"Mack got upset. He told the bloke off, showed him up in front of his mates. Black, he was. His mates called him *Tyson*, because he could handle himself. We found out later his name was Trevor Williamson. *Trevor John Williamson, twenty-four years old, a shop assistant from Norwood*. Anyway this bloke glared at Mack for the next hour, like he was working himself up. Mack could see him. I told him we should go but he said, *No, let's have a bit of a laugh.*

Kenny imagined Mack leaning against the bar wearing the kind of suit that he'd been wearing on the day he'd saved him from Tibbs and his mates at Stratford Station.

"Mack was drinking a lot, more than usual. He kept saying, *Is he looking? Is he still looking?* I told him to leave it. The man had a bunch of mates with him. But Mack didn't move, just leaned against the bar, downing shorts, looking round at Tyson every now and then. Just before four they started to go. This Tyson, he passed right by Mack. He must have swore or said something because Mack swallowed his drink, buttoned up his suit jacket and followed him out."

Kenny was listening intently to Spenser but he was distracted for a moment by Mack outside talking to Tommy Fortune. Tommy had appeared out of nowhere, wearing a huge oversized coat that almost touched the ground. Tommy was pointing down to a zip-up holdall he was carrying. Kenny raised his eyebrows. Tommy really did know everyone.

"I followed Mack out of the pub," Spenser went on. "I had no choice. There was about five of them. The funny thing was, once we got outside, they didn't want to know, they all started walking backwards down the street. Giving us the hard-man looks. They didn't want to fight though. Except for Tyson. He started mouthing off. Mack just stood there. He called Mack a coward and turned to follow his mates. Mack jumped him from behind. His mates were too far away and Tyson was just sprawled out on the ground. Mack stepped back. That was enough for him. But Tyson jumped up to face up to Mack with a knife in his hand."

Kenny pictured a flick-knife. He'd seen kids in school with them. Outside Mack was deep in conversation with Tommy.

"Mack took one look at this knife and went mad. Madder than I've ever seen him. He kicked out at the bloke's hand, like in the films. I remember thinking, *When did Mack get into martial arts?* Tyson's knife dropped on the ground. Mack was down in a shot and so was Tyson. They were both fumbling on the ground for it. The bloke's mates had started to drift back towards us. They couldn't see what was going on. Only I could see. I kept saying to Mack, *Leave it! Leave it!*

"Mack got the knife. Tyson put his hands up, like they do in films, as if Mack had a gun. The bloke had had enough. He wasn't doing nothing else. One of his mates was like five metres away. He was swearing and stuff but he was backing off. I been in enough fights. I know when a bloke's had enough."

Spenser stopped and seemed to be thinking hard. He rubbed at the tattoo on his arm, his hairs standing up, the word *Mandy* clear under the lights.

"What happened?" Kenny whispered.

"Mack stabbed him."

Kenny was silent. Spenser's face had a pinched look about it, his lips puckered up.

"Afterwards Mack said he was afraid that the bloke's mates would come with their knives but I never read the situation like that. It was just Tyson who wanted trouble. And he had finished. I couldn't believe it at first. I thought Mack had pocketed the knife and was giving Tyson a punch in the guts to remember him by. But then there was all this blood. It was sick."

"Did the police believe him?" Kenny said.

Outside Mack and Tommy Fortune were laughing about something and Mack was handing him some money and taking something tiny from Tommy's other hand. He'd just bought some dope, Kenny was sure.

"Mack told the police it was self-defence. It was Tyson's knife, see. His mates agreed that it was his knife." Spenser's voice had dropped to a whisper again. "Mack said that he'd tried to pick it up to stop Tyson using it on him. And that the stabbing had happened in the scuffle."

"An accident?" Kenny said, frowning.

"Only it wasn't. I saw it," Spenser said, raising his eyebrows. "The thing is, Mack's a hard man. You don't want to cross him. He's got a temper. He does things on the spur of the moment. Then he regrets them."

"What did you tell the police?" Kenny said.

"That it was an accident. It happened during the scuffle for the knife. I backed Mack up. He's my mate."

"What about the others. Tyson's mates?"

"They didn't see that much and anyway you imagine the scene. Two well-dressed white men facing five black blokes, all a bit drunk. One of them has his own knife and threatens to use it. The white bloke, good job, lives with his parents, defends himself. We spent all evening at the police station. They let us go home in the end but we had to let the police know about our whereabouts and stuff. They called Mack and me in every couple of weeks for a few months. Going over and over our story. In the end they said they'd leave it to the Crown Prosecution Service to decide if there was enough evidence for a charge of manslaughter. It all came to nothing in the end."

"And Mack felt bad?"

Kenny was watching Mack walk back towards the café. Tommy Fortune was following. The coat was huge, hanging off his shoulders. It was for a much bigger man.

"It's hard to tell with Mack. It's not like we talked about it much."

The door opened and Mack came in. "What you two talking about?"

"Hello, Spense," Tommy Fortune said. "I know you. Joe Harris's brother, right?"

Kenny nodded.

"We were talking about football," Spenser said.

"What's the grub like in here?" Mack asked Kenny. "I'm feeling peckish."

"It's all right," Kenny said.

"I'll get some chips," he said, standing up, pulling his wallet out of his back pocket. "Want some, Tommy?"

"Go on then, twist my arm!"

When Mack and Tommy walked towards the counter Spenser leaned forward and spoke softly.

"Mack said he was sorry it happened. But I tell you what. He kept the shirt he was wearing. Covered in blood it was, but he's never washed it. I saw it in a bag in the boot of the car only the other week."

"Why?" Kenny asked.

"A sort of trophy?" Spenser said, shrugging his shoulders. "Listen, Kenny, he's my best mate, but I wouldn't get on the wrong side of him. He likes you, but don't ever take the mick out of him, or let him down. I never have."

Mack came back to the table with a plate of chips.

"Help yourself," he said.

Kenny shook his head. He had no appetite.

FOURTEEN
NATALIE

Joe replied immediately with a text. It came just moments after Natalie had sent her message. It was as if he'd been awake waiting for her to contact him. She read his message over a couple of times.

Dear Natalie, Kenny went out. I don't know where. He doesn't tell me stuff. How are you? Did you get my letter?

She dropped the mobile on to the duvet. Now what? Should she answer it?

The second text came a couple of minutes later.

Natalie, there's a place that Kenny goes to late at night. If you're worried we could go and find him. I've got the car. It's no trouble.

She didn't know what to do. Maybe Kenny had seen Jimmy Mackintosh by now and everything was sorted out. On the other hand the man had beaten Kenny up. His messages sounded *threatening*. If Kenny had gone to meet him, did it mean more trouble?

Jimmy Mackintosh. She remembered him from

months ago; that night on Stratford Station when those lads had picked on Kenny. She had run off to find a member of staff and must have passed him. Not that she'd noticed at the time because she'd been frantic. When she'd returned, pulling a hapless London Transport worker behind her, she'd seen him, standing straight, looking like someone who had come from a wedding reception. He had seen off the teenagers and was helping Kenny up. He'd been nice, caring, she remembered.

Why had he turned against Kenny?

Kenny had been mates with him for a while, Natalie knew that. During the weeks that they had been together Kenny had often been dropped off in a dark blue BMW that was driven by Jimmy Mackintosh. He'd been to a football match and clubbing and drinking in pubs. Sometimes, he told her, they just drove around for the sake of it.

It had annoyed Natalie from time to time. Kenny was often later than he said. Sometimes he came to her and left early because he said he had to meet Jimmy Mackintosh. She wanted to complain but found it difficult to stay angry with Kenny once he'd arrived. What was the point of arguing? Kenny wasn't always at her beck and call. Maybe that's why she was so keen on him.

One night he hadn't turned up at all and they'd rowed the next time she'd seen him.

"You're always out with Jimmy Mackintosh! Don't you think I'd like to go out?" she'd said, her arms folded across her chest.

"We said we wouldn't go out. Not until my brother knows about us. Anyway, you know I'm broke. Mack pays for me when we go out!"

Kenny lay back on her bed. Natalie sat stiffly on the edge.

"I don't know why you bother. He's old!"

"He's twenty-five. Age has got nothing to do with it. He's a laugh! I like hanging round with him and Spenser."

"What about Russell and your other mates?"

"I've seen them around. Thing is I like Mack. He's got a car. It's different to being with Russell and the others. They want to know what I'm up to and it's not like I can tell them."

"You mean about me?"

Kenny put his hand out and pulled her towards him.

"I can't exactly boast about you, can I?"

"And what about Jimmy Mackintosh?" she said, letting herself be pulled along.

"He doesn't know about Joe or you, and in any case I don't have to explain stuff to him. We just have a laugh."

"But what does he want?" she said, half-lying across him. "Doesn't it seem funny to you? A twenty-five year old wanting to hang out with a sixteen year old? You don't think. . . He's not *gay*, is he?"

Kenny's face fell into a grin.

"Don't be ridiculous!" he said, rolling over so that she was trapped underneath him.

"Get off," she'd said, laughing. "You're smothering me!"

That had been weeks before. She'd had to get used to Jimmy Mackintosh's presence.

Kenny's mobile beeped again, the sound like an exclamation mark in the quiet room. It was another message from Joe.

Shall I come round? I can be there in fifteen minutes.

Natalie didn't want Joe to come round, she was sure of that. If she was honest, she didn't want to see Joe ever again. It wasn't that she *hated* him. It was just that any mention of him reminded her of those days when she was deceiving him.

She got up and went to her desk. Behind her computer was a noticeboard with a calendar pinned to it. It was showing the month of December, and on the seventh she'd written the words *Kenny's birthday*. She took it off the wall. Flicking back through it she came to the page for October. Beside the second she'd written *Joe goes back to uni*.

How innocent the dates looked on paper. The beginning of their affair, and the day it had become public knowledge. For eight weeks she'd clung on to Kenny while pretending she was still Joe's girlfriend. It was easy because Joe wasn't actually at her side. He was two hundred and fifty miles away in Durham. As well as sending her letters Joe would ring once a week and talk for ages about what he was doing. She'd listen, but all the while she was thinking about Kenny.

What had happened to her desire for Joe? Joe who wanted to *STOP POVERTY NOW!* Joe, who spoke with fervour about debt and hunger. Joe, who seemed so different from anyone else she had ever met.

It had seeped away.

Joe hadn't seemed to notice. As she cooled off he became more passionate. They'd never actually had sex, but the closer he got to returning to uni the further he pushed it with her.

His parents said she could spend the last night with him, in his bedroom. Joe was excited, passionate. *We're ready*, he'd said. *We're a real couple*, he'd said, *this is serious*. But she'd changed by then. She no longer wanted him, so she made excuses. She was afraid of becoming pregnant. She didn't want to do it in his parents' house. She wanted to wait until her exams were over. He agreed. They went to bed and she lay wide awake by his side. She knew then it was all over between them.

Just after two she'd heard the front door bang shut, then footsteps on the stairs. It was Kenny, she knew. An odd feeling came over her. She threw the duvet back and twisted and turned on the sheet, moving her pillow to different angles so that she could get comfortable. Her legs were restless, her nightie felt too tight, she was too hot, too bothered.

She liked Kenny. He was her boyfriend's brother. Why shouldn't she like him? But it was more than that. He was funny and confident. He could find a laugh in just about anything. He rolled his eyes behind Joe's back when he was arguing about politics. He liked movies. He loaned her DVDs of directors he liked and talked to her about them. He was going to travel, he said, across the USA in a Greyhound bus, stopping at the places where his favourite movies were set.

You need proper money for that, Joe always said, throwing a bucket of water over Kenny's words.

Kenny made her smile. He also made her skin tingle if he touched her accidentally. Something he seemed to do whenever she saw him. A hand on her arm, the tips of his fingers on her shoulder, cupping her elbows as he passed behind her along the hallway, his breath on her neck.

That night, Joe's last night before he went to university, she tossed and turned and eventually got up and went downstairs to the kitchen to get some water. Standing at the sink she looked down and realized that her nightie was almost see-through, and she folded one arm across her breasts to cover herself. The door opened behind her and Kenny stood there.

"Hi!" she said, embarrassed at her near-nakedness.

He didn't answer. He just stared at her, his eyes heavy, his mouth open.

"Are you all right?" she said, putting the glass of water down on the draining board.

He walked across and put his arms around her and pulled her close to him, his face in her hair, her face against his chest. He felt hot and his hand gripped her back so that she almost couldn't breathe.

Then he kissed her.

Afterwards she went back up to Joe's bed and got in beside him. *I'll come round your house tomorrow after Joe's gone*, Kenny had said. She lay in the dark, her eyes wide open, her heart thumping in her chest. It was too loud, she thought, pushing against it with her fist, it would wake Joe up and he would know what she had done.

She had fallen in love.

Why hadn't she told Joe? Eight weeks of lying to him. Why?

She didn't want him to arrive on her doorstep and try to persuade her to change her mind. She knew that he would do it. That his hasty, unplanned visit might burst the bubble of pleasure she was in. So she put it off. She kept telling herself that she would tell him the next week or the week after, when she was more secure with Kenny, when she really felt that they were a couple. But she never really felt that, and if she was honest that had been part of the thrill.

There never had been a right time to tell Joe.

So Kenny blurted it out on the day of his birthday.

Natalie put the calendar back on the wall. She walked back to the bed and saw Kenny's mobile light up. "Not Joe again," she said through clenched teeth. The name *Mack* showed on the screen. She put it to her ear and listened.

Don't think you'll be able to get away from me. I'll find you, Kenny. I'll search every street in East London. If you let me down now I'll never forget it and when I've finished with you you won't forget it either. By six o'clock. The Sugar House. I expect you to be there.

She listened again. The words were virtually the same as the earlier messages, but the voice sounded slurred and angry. *If you let me down. . .* The tone was one of desperation. What had Kenny got himself into?

She rang Joe. Then she turned Kenny's mobile off. She'd heard enough messages for one night.

Twenty minutes later she was dressed in jeans, boots, fleece, puffa jacket, hat and gloves. She opened the front door as quietly as she could, and waited as the red Ford came rushing down the street and pulled up outside her house.

FIFTEEN

Tommy Fortune woke up. Kenny watched as he sat up slowly, stretched his free arm up to the ceiling and looked around as though he had no idea where he was. He pulled himself up to a sitting position and tugged at the sling on his injured arm as though it was too tight. He looked at Kenny and frowned.

"You still here, mate?" he said.

Kenny nodded.

"I feel rubbish," Tommy said, his hand cupping the side of his face. Then he slumped sideways, his head on the arm of the sofa.

"Who hit you?" Kenny said.

"Don't remember," Tommy said. "Story of my life, that."

"What about a cup of tea?" Kenny said, briskly. "Or coffee?"

He didn't want Tommy to fall asleep again. He had almost an hour and a half. It wasn't far to the docks but

104

he still had to persuade him and then physically get him there, which would mean a cab.

Tommy hadn't answered so he stood up and gave him a gentle shake.

"I'll make some tea, shall I? And then I'll tell you about the iPods," he said.

"Two sugars," Tommy mumbled.

Kenny found the kitchen. He clicked the light switch and looked with dismay at the pile of dishes on the drainer. Some still had food stuck to them. The remains of a sliced loaf was on the side and beside it an opened tub of butter which looked yellow and greasy. An encrusted knife lay beside it and half a tomato. Kenny grimaced with distaste. The bin was over-flowing and on the floor, by its side, was a cat litter tray with cat crap in it. He stepped gingerly around it and reached up to a cupboard to look for the tea bags. He picked up the kettle and filled it up at the sink, edging it between upturned pots that were soaking in brown water.

He paused. Actually he wasn't feeling too well. His head was starting to ache, his hand felt like a bowling ball and his thigh was hurting. He needed more painkillers. Maybe Tommy had some that the hospital had given him. He put the cold tap on and cupped his good hand underneath it. He carried the water up to his forehead three or four times. It woke him up a bit. Now wasn't the time to start feeling sorry for himself. He rummaged round and found two mugs and some milk in the fridge that looked OK. While he was getting rid of the tea bags he heard movement from the living room. When he went in Tommy was sitting up smoking a cigarette.

"Here you are!" Kenny said, placing Tommy's mug on the floor beside him.

Before Tommy could say anything Kenny burst out with his story about the iPods again. This man, he said, rushing his words so that Tommy wouldn't interrupt, had ten brand-new iPods, still in the boxes. He was letting them go for thirty quid each. He wanted rid of them asap. He was getting a flight in the morning from Docklands Airport. He needed quick cash. Kenny had made him promise that he would save them for Tommy.

Tommy listened, his mug of tea covering the bottom of his face.

"Thirty quid each?" he said, thoughtfully.

"You could knock them out for three times that, maybe more."

"What's in it for you?"

Kenny paused. He'd expected Tommy to say something like this.

"Bloke's giving me a few quid. And, I was thinking, you could throw a few DVDs my way. Say, *Godfather* trilogy? *Pulp Fiction*?"

Kenny already had the movies but it sounded good enough.

Tommy looked as though he was weighing it up. He drained his cup and then placed it back on the floor.

"Ten iPods. It's bad timing. I've just had painkillers. The last thing I feel like doing is going out. . ."

He lay on his side again, his head awkwardly propped on the arm of the chair.

"Tommy, this is a good deal!"

"I don't get it," Tommy said. "Why you're so bothered."

"Thing is," Kenny said, a feeling of anxiety descending on to him, "I kind of boasted to this bloke that I knew someone really *professional*. That's why he's waiting. If you don't show it looks bad on me."

Tommy closed his eyes. Kenny waited. He couldn't look desperate, otherwise Tommy would suspect something. On the other hand he had to keep going. If Tommy didn't come of his own free will he would get the blame. Mack had made that clear.

"I think you're trying to pull a fast one on me," Tommy said, suddenly, his words clear and crisp even though he was slumped on the sofa, his eyes still closed.

"How come?" Kenny said.

The room was very quiet. From outside Kenny could hear the patter of rain or snow on the window. From inside he could hear the blood throbbing through his head. Did Tommy know something? Was that what he meant? He'd seen Kenny with Mack, before in the café. Did he know that Mack had plans for him?

"I'm just telling you what this bloke said," Kenny said, his voice thick with uncertainty. "Ten iPods. I thought you'd be interested."

"How do I know they're any good? They might be duds. It's not like I can take them back."

Tommy sat up, looking fresher than before. He leaned

107

his good elbow on one knee. He looked straight at Kenny. Kenny went to speak but faltered. He looked away, afraid that his composure might crumble under Tommy's scrutiny. He stared down at the magazines on the floor. He picked one up. *World War Two*. Was Tommy *reading* them?

"A hobby of mine," Tommy said. "War against the Nazis. My granddad died on the last day of the war. Can you believe that? The day before VE day. Seventh May 1945. He managed to stay alive from 1939. Six years of fighting and dodging bullets and then the day before the peace he got shot by his own side. Accidental death."

Kenny nodded, flicking the page.

"I like reading about the war. I didn't know my granddad but he was an unlucky bastard. I like to find out what he might have been doing."

Kenny replaced the magazine on top of the pile. He looked back at Tommy, his face completely still. He stood up, brushing his jeans down with his good hand.

"Don't matter about the iPods," he said. "There's someone else I know. Forget it. You have a sleep."

"Wait, wait, wait. . ." Tommy said. "No need to get the hump. I'm just careful, I know you're doing me a favour. Course I want them. And you can come to my lock-up tomorrow. I'm sure I've got some *Pulp Fiction* sets. Not sure about the others. . . Course I want the iPods. I'm a businessman. It's what I do. I just need to go. . ." Tommy pointed towards the hallway. "You sit down. I'm just off to the bog."

Tommy used his good arm to pat Kenny on the

shoulder. Kenny sat down again. He had persuaded Tommy. *He had done it*. He lifted up his bad hand and started to unwind the bandage that Nat had put on it. It was sopping wet and loose. When it was off he held his hand close to the radiator and felt the heat on his skin.

It was up to him now to try and change the course of events. He had to concentrate. He wouldn't just deliver Tommy to Mack like a parcel of goods. He had to *think*.

He pictured Mack sitting in his car, parked outside the Sugar House. Maybe he'd be drinking from a can of lager. Mack would be tense, unhappy, waiting to see if Kenny would do what he was told. Maybe he'd get tea from the café. Maybe he'd even go into the club for half an hour to pass the time. He'd be on his own, that was for sure, looking at his watch, looking at his mobile, waiting for a message. All the time he'd be thinking about Kenny and what he was doing.

Mack was depending on Kenny. Mack needed Kenny. It meant that, for a while at least, Kenny had the upper hand.

He would try and persuade Mack that there was another way. If he brought Tommy along maybe Mack and he could talk to him. Tommy Fortune was no hero. He wasn't going to go to the law if it meant he was going to be in physical danger. Surely Mack could see that?

And on top of that there was the matter of five thousand pounds. Would Tommy Fortune really turn that down in favour of a beating?

109

As if by magic Tommy appeared at the door wearing the giant overcoat. He also had one of his dicky bows on. He saw Kenny looking at it.

"Gotta look smart, lad," he said.

"Where's the sling?" Kenny said, seeing both of Tommy's hands poking out of the sleeves of the heavy coat.

"It's easier like this. It was just a sprain."

Kenny got his mobile out. "I'll call a cab."

"Nope." Tommy shook his head and walked out of the flat. "Got to go round my mum's first."

Kenny stopped.

"The money. I haven't got three hundred smackers here, mate. I don't keep a penny here."

The money! Kenny had forgotten that Tommy would need the money for the iPods. For pity's sake, why hadn't he thought of that? Stupid! Stupid!

He followed Tommy out on to the landing and waited while he pulled the door shut quietly.

"Thieves round every corner here. I keep my money at my mum's. She don't live far. We'll still get there in time."

It was snowing outside. Kenny zipped his jacket up and tucked his bad hand up his sleeve. He looked at the early-morning sky. It was jet black. In the distance he heard the buzz of a motorbike. It came closer, reaching a pitch, then it receded until he could hear it no more.

The street was empty, a thin dusting of white on the pavements. The only footprints were those of Tommy ahead of him. He walked quickly, aware of a hot wringing pain in his thigh. He'd forgotten to ask Tommy for the painkillers.

"Come on, lad," Tommy said turning back. "We don't want to miss our meeting!"

Kenny quickened his pace. *It would be all right.*

SIXTEEN
BEING MATES WITH MACK

Kenny was wary of Mack. His memories of the fight in the old bread warehouse and Spenser's story had given him an uncomfortable feeling, and he avoided contact. Mack had helped him on Stratford station and was good company, Kenny had to agree, but this other side of Mack, this dark side, put him on his guard. A few days after the South London match Kenny came home from school to find a note under his door from Mack asking him to give him a call if he wanted to go to another game the following week. Kenny called and said he couldn't make it. After that Mack sent him a couple of texts and he sent polite, wooden replies.

In any case, he had the situation with Natalie to sort out.

It was two weeks since his brother Joe had returned to university and Kenny was on his way to Nat's as he had been most evenings since that first night. Walking slowly, pausing to look in shop windows, he wondered what on earth he was doing. A couple of times he almost stopped and turned round. He had other places to go; the Scarlet Lady; his mate Russell's; the cinema. He had new DVDs to watch; he even had schoolwork to do. He continued walking though, his head dipping, his shoulders rounded, his feet carrying him to somewhere he shouldn't go.

He thought of that first night, that first shocking kiss. Why had he done it? To see if he could? To see if she would? When he flung open the kitchen door that night he had been on a kind of high, his nerves still reverberating from the football fight and his thoughts jangling with the news that Mack had actually killed a man.

And there she was. By the sink, holding a glass of water, her nightshirt loose, her arm covering her breasts. She looked at him with her mouth open. He could feel something from her. She didn't speak but he felt her pull him in, draw him close, and then his eyes were shut and he sank into her mouth and that was the start.

He should have left it there. He should have treated it as a kind of dare. As if he dared himself to steal one of his brother's books or CDs. To see if he could do it. Once he'd done it, what was the point in going back for more?

He'd intended to tell her, the next evening, at her house, that it would go no further. They'd only kissed. He'd pulled her close and felt her tiny breasts up against his chest and her hips clinging to him but it had only been a kiss. Nothing more.

He arrived later than he'd said. Her parents were out and she pulled him by the hand up the stairs to her bedroom. He'd sat down awkwardly in a chair by the window and cleared his throat a couple of times. She was sitting cross-legged on the bed, her hands clasped. They were only a few steps apart. There was music playing but he had no idea who it was. His head was full of words he wanted to say, things he wanted to do.

Her face was shiny and every now and then she gave a little shrug as if to say, *What do we do now?* When she got up to change the CD he grabbed hold of her hand and pulled her to him. She resisted and he knew that was his chance. To do the right thing. To walk away from her before Joe found out any of it.

"I was going to finish it with him," she said, her face close to his. "As soon as he went back to uni. I was going to ring him and tell him it was over."

That was it. She hadn't wanted Joe anyway. Kenny felt himself swooning, and stumbled towards the bed, drawing her with him. She was much smaller than him and he made sure he wasn't crushing her as he kissed her over and over. He felt her hands push up his T-shirt and pull at his belt. He pushed his face into her neck and smelled her skin as his head and shoulders and body stiffened.

Kenny had had sex twice. Once when he was fifteen. The second time in the summer, a couple of months before. Both times were at parties, in an upstairs toilet and in a corner of a back garden. One minute he'd been kissing and touching a willing and friendly girl. The next minute buttons and zips and hooks had come undone and they were struggling in some kind of intoxicated wrestling match. The first time it had only taken seconds and they'd used the toilet paper to clean up. The second time he'd used a condom. In the dark shadows of the garden, he'd pulled the tiny packet from his pocket and somehow managed to fiddle it into place before he'd lost interest in the whole thing. The girl, Bev, was eager and clung to him with her arms and legs. She was much more experienced and held him in the corner of the dark garden with her deep kisses and soft hands. Afterwards she'd given him her mobile number but he'd never used it.

Lying beside Nat, his legs entangled in her bedclothes, he almost laughed out loud.

"I'll tell Joe we're finished tomorrow," Nat said, decisively. "But I won't mention you."

While Nat was in the bathroom washing, Kenny got dressed. As he pulled his clothes on he felt a tight ball of guilt in his chest. For pity's sake, Joe was his *brother*. Joe always the golden boy, Kenny always the awkward one. Joe the high flyer while Kenny slouched along at street level. There were loads of girls around. Why did Kenny choose to have the one that belonged to Joe?

"I'll phone him tomorrow," Nat whispered.

They were kissing again, Nat's shoulders were wet from the shower, her towel damp. She seemed to disappear into Kenny's arms and he realized that maybe it was her who had chosen him.

She hadn't told Joe, though. In two weeks she still hadn't told him.

Turning into her street Kenny knew that he should end it with her. Whether she told Joe or not, it just wasn't right. At her front door he paused before ringing the bell. He would tell her it was over. In his head he had the words, *I don't want to see you any more*. It was simple, it was easy, then he could get back to his regular life.

The sound of footsteps coming towards the door made his heart thump with anticipation. His resolve crumbled. She opened the door and her face beamed up at him. She had a tight yellow T-shirt on and her hair was sticking up on top. He wanted to reach out and smooth it down. She went on tiptoes and kissed him on the mouth. It made his skin tingle.

He couldn't give her up.

He went in and closed the door quietly behind him.

Hours later, walking along the high road, he heard the tooting of a car horn. He looked round. It was a BMW and Mack was driving. He walked across to the car.

"Jump in, I'll give you a lift home!" Mack said.

"It's not far," Kenny said.

"Come on. I'll tell you about this new car I'm looking at."

Kenny didn't know what to do. It would be rude to just walk away.

"Brand new. Twenty grand. Fifteen if I get it off the Internet!"

Mack reached across and threw open the passenger door. Kenny got in. It was late and he was tired. It didn't mean he had to hang around with Mack again. Mack turned the music off and drove. He talked about the car he wanted, the colour, the model, the specifications.

"You missed a good match last week," he said, changing the subject.

"I couldn't make it," Kenny said.

"No fighting," Mack said. "That's only for special matches."

Kenny nodded.

"It's just a sort of game we play."

"Didn't look much like a game to me," Kenny said, lightly.

There was quiet in the car. Kenny sensed that Mack wanted to say something to him.

"Where you been? Out with Spenser?" he said to break the tension.

"Up Epping. There's a pub we like up there, the Huntsman. You should come."

Kenny didn't answer. They were close to the square in which he lived.

"Spenser said he told you about the trouble I had a couple of years ago? With the black kid from Norwood?"

Kenny nodded. The car pulled into his square and slid quietly past the wine merchants and round the small garden in the middle. It stopped a few doors along from his house.

"You don't want to take too much notice of what

Spenser said. He exaggerates. He's famous for it. He likes a bit of drama."

"He said. . ." Kenny stopped. He wanted to say, *He said you stabbed someone. . .*

"It was an accident. The black kid had the knife. We struggled. He got stabbed. That was it. Spenser likes to tell it different but that was the way it was."

Kenny didn't know what to say. He put his hand on the door handle.

"I'll bet Spenser made it a big secret when he told you," Mack said, shaking his head. "I'll bet he said, *Don't tell Mack I told you!* I'm right, aren't I?"

Kenny nodded.

"He told me about your reaction as soon as we dropped you off. *The kid's jaw nearly fell off when I told him about Tyson*, he said. See what I mean? He loves a bit of drama. Take no notice. It was an accident. The police didn't press charges. Spenser likes to think of me as some kind of *hard man*. He's the softie with the wife and kid and I'm the tough guy. But it's all bollocks."

"Right. . ." Kenny didn't know what to say.

"Tomorrow night, we're going to the dogs. Spenser's bringing his kid, sweet little thing she is. Come along. I'll pick you up. Seven?"

Kenny opened the door to get out. He had said he'd go round Nat's the next night.

"Seven all right?" Mack said.

He nodded. Why not? He stood on the pavement and watched the car drive off. The dogs. It would give him a break from seeing Nat.

A couple of days after the trip to the dogs Mack picked Kenny up outside his school.

"Fancy something to eat?" he said.

They had pizza and Mack paid. Spenser joined them and they went for a drive to Epping and had a few drinks in the Huntsman. Then Mack drove stupidly through the narrow forest lanes, turning this way and that, speeding up, slowing down, braking suddenly so that they fell forward. *Too fast*, Spenser shouted, several times, but Mack just laughed. Afterwards Kenny asked Mack to drop him off at Nat's.

A few days later Kenny took his *Godfather* DVDs and they watched them in Mack's house, on his parent's flat-screen TV. Spenser had a bag full of boxes of perfume. *Duty free, out-of-date stock,* he'd said, grinning. He offered Kenny one, *A fiver to you*, he said but Kenny shook his head. He had no idea what sort of perfume Nat wore and in any case he didn't want to buy her stuff that had been knocked off. Spenser shrugged good-naturedly and gave a running commentary on famous scenes in *The Godfather* while Mack sat silently, drinking from can after can of lager.

Kenny started to enjoy himself. He didn't want to go to football again, but he didn't mind driving round in Mack's car sitting behind Mack and Spenser, heading for places that Mack liked to go. In the space behind Mack's seat was a coolbox and there were always cans of lager. *Help yourself!* Mack said.

One night, Mack's girlfriend Kelly was in the front seat. She turned round and gave Kenny a regal wave.

She had dark hair and deep red lipstick. The smell of her perfume filled the car and Kenny could see her nails, long and patterned. Mack dropped her off at her friend's house and she stood by the driver's door, leaned down and kissed Mack on the lips, a tiny peck and then she walked away, her tight skirt showing the shape of her backside.

"Your eyes are on stalks!" Mack had said and Kenny felt himself go red.

They picked Spenser up and then Kenny asked Mack to drop him off at Nat's house.

"Don't you ever take your girlfriend out?" Mack said.

"Too tight," Spenser said.

"Or she looks like Miss Piggy," Mack said.

"Or one of the Ugly Sisters," Spenser joined in.

They continued listing odd characters and Kenny found himself folding his arms, irritated at their immaturity. They left him at the end of Nat's street. He walked away.

"Got the hump?" Mack shouted.

He didn't turn round. They'd annoyed him with their stupid comments. Maybe he didn't need Mack and Spenser. Maybe he would avoid them, get back to his own crowd. There was a lot of stuff he could do. He didn't need to be hanging around with a couple of overgrown teenagers.

The next day he found his old mate Russell sitting in his usual seat in the Scarlet Lady. He was surrounded by some other kids that Kenny had been friendly with. He sat on the fringes of the group and listened to them talk and joke and gossip. He bought Russell a drink and they chatted quietly about school and people they knew. Russell seemed interested in what Kenny had been doing.

"Somebody said you were hanging round with an older bloke."

Kenny nodded.

"In a BMW?"

"One year old," Kenny said.

"What's his story then? Don't say he *fancies* you!"

Kenny sighed. Maybe this was the reason he'd stopped hanging about with kids his own age.

"No, he doesn't! He's not gay. Neither am I!"

"No, right. I didn't mean that you were. I was only joking!"

After another drink he went home early and watched the beginning of *Pulp Fiction* again. About ten his mum knocked on his room door. Her face had an expression of disapproval on it.

"That older guy for you. Jimmy Mack. It's really too late to go out now. Remember it's school tomorrow."

He went downstairs feeling mildly irked at his mum's tone. Mack and Spenser were standing at his front door, looking awkward.

"How do you fancy coming to this nightclub, down at the docks?" Mack said.

"It's a bit late," Kenny said.

"What's up. Got school in the morning?" Mack said.

"Course he's got school!" Spenser said. "Let's leave it."

"We'll tell you what it was like," Mack said, turning away.

Kenny looked back into the house. He could hear the sound of the television from the living room. Upstairs *Pulp Fiction* was frozen on his screen.

"Hang on!" he said.

It's school tomorrow – as if he cared. He picked up his jacket and followed Mack and Spenser out to the car.

SEVENTEEN
SUNDAY, 18 DECEMBER, 4.55 A.M.

Tommy Fortune's mother lived a couple of streets away.

Kenny followed as Tommy marched ahead in his great-coat, the snow melting away in his footsteps. He looked at the time. Just over an hour left. Six o'clock was looming up ahead of him. He plodded after Tommy through the empty streets and felt the minutes slipping by, racing by. When he'd been at Nat's, or even at home, the night seemed to stretch ahead of him like a long dark road. Now morning was just round the corner. He looked up at the sky. It was still pitch dark, and yet there was something, a smell or a feeling of freshness, something that hinted at morning.

Then, one way or another, it would be all over.

Turning a corner Tommy made a sudden stop. He put his hand up to halt Kenny. Then he edged back behind a parked van and waited. A moment later a police car crunched by. It was driving slowly, as if looking for somebody. Kenny felt his stomach ripple. Tommy was in a crouching position and stayed still until it had passed by.

"Last thing I need," he said, standing up straight. "This detective I know. *Sullivan*. He's got it in for me. Always cruising around, looking for me, picking me up for nothing. I thought it might be him."

Picking him up for *nothing*. Kenny bit his lip. Tommy was always in some sort of trouble. Receiving stolen goods, stealing, drugs. Joe had told him about Tommy Fortune's past. He'd spent a few years here and there in prison.

"The trouble with the law is that they always think the worst of you!" Tommy said, in a loud whisper.

They walked on, Kenny smiling wryly at the irony of this statement.

"Here we are!" Tommy said.

"I'll wait here," Kenny said.

Tommy disappeared into the house.

Kenny leaned against the front garden wall. The cold fresh air was making him feel better. He had found Tommy. He was taking Tommy to Mack. But he was not just going to hand him over. He was going to make a stand, to force Mack to do it his way.

The words *force Mack* sat uneasy in his head. Could Mack be forced? He looked down at Tommy's mother's front garden wall. It was wet with loose snow. He put his hand on it and then lifted his wet palm on his forehead. There was just a tingle of pain from his broken skin.

Mack was stronger than him and Tommy put together. It wasn't his *physical* strength that was the problem, although that was dangerous enough in itself. Kenny looked at his bad hand, the skin naked and exposed after hours of being bandaged up. It was Mack's strength of mind that was the problem. Once he'd decided something there was no going back, it seemed.

But Kenny had something to bargain with.

He pulled the letter from his back pocket. It was beginning to look battered, its edges curling, a deep fold where he'd had to double it so that it would go into his pocket. He would tell Mack that he'd written this letter and that he'd given it to a friend to look after. If anything happened to him then the friend was to post it. He imagined himself saying that to Mack. *If you hurt me my friend will post the letter. Then you won't have to worry about Tommy any more because the police will know the truth about Jon Tibbs.*

Jon Tibbs. It was the first time Kenny had thought about him in hours. He pictured him, on Stratford station, his small round glasses making him look like a boffin. He'd shown Kenny no mercy that night.

Kenny closed his eyes, his mood crumbling, his head full of darkness. A car in the forest, a boy with glasses running away, crashing into bushes and trees. Then nothing, just silence.

The front door opened suddenly and a woman in a red dressing gown stood there beside Tommy. Kenny took a couple of steps into the shadows. He slid his letter back where it came from. Tommy was talking to his mother but Kenny couldn't hear much of what was being said. The woman's voice had a distressed tone to it

125

and she was reaching up and touching Tommy's eye. She was patting his arm and fussing over him.

A black cab came into the street. Kenny watched it approaching. It pulled up a couple of metres away. Tommy must have ordered it. He looked at it gratefully.

Tommy's mum's dressing gown was engulfing him. It gave Kenny a twist of anguish. Why did he have to come here? Why hadn't he made up a story about the man not wanting his money immediately?

The front door slammed shut and Tommy walked across to Kenny.

"God!" he said. "Mothers! Is yours like that?"

It wasn't really a question. Kenny followed Tommy into the cab.

"Put your seatbelt on!" Tommy said, cheerfully. "Don't want to break the law, do we?"

Kenny gave a weak smile and pulled the belt across with his good hand.

EIGHTEEN
CLUBBING WITH MACK

"Are you sure they'll let me in here?" Kenny said.

The car pulled up outside the club. The words THE SUGAR HOUSE were in purple neon lights that shone out amongst the gloomy warehouses and building sites of West India Quays.

"When's your birthday?"

"Two weeks next Wednesday," Kenny said, after a moment's calculation. "I'll be seventeen."

"So you're sweet sixteen," said Spenser.

"Never been kissed," said Mack.

"I'll bet he's been kissed a few times, haven't you, Kenny?"

Spenser turned round and grinned at him. Kenny sighed and sat back in the car seat.

Spenser had been full of chat all the way there. He'd been talking about some scam at the airport. The words *designer gear* and *twenty-two carat gold* and *easy money* had drifted across him, but he hadn't really been

127

listening. He wondered what he was doing there, in the car, with these two jokers. Somehow or other he'd been drawn into Mack and Spenser's lives. One minute he liked them. The next he was annoyed by them. Why did he hang around with them? Because they kept him busy? Took him away from the things that bothered him? Like the situation with Nat and Joe? Maybe it all went back to that day on Stratford station when Jon Tibbs and his mates took advantage. That was the thing, the tie. Mack had *saved* him.

They walked into the Sugar House without any questions. Kenny wasn't surprised. He looked older than his years. It was Mack and Spenser who were giggling like schoolboys.

The club was really just a series of bars with different seating and lighting in each room. There was a chillout room with low settees where the scent of dope was strong. There were a couple of bars with smart chairs and a widescreen TV showing clips of football matches interspersed with movie and music clips. There was a room where people were dancing with earsplitting music and girls in skimpy clothes, their breasts jiggling up and down. It made Mack and Spenser look and laugh for ages, making disparaging or sexual comments. The three of them ended up in the bar with the big screen. They sat in a corner where some women were. Mack seemed to know them and he offered Kenny as their *toy boy*. A dark-haired woman of about thirty sat down beside Kenny and put one arm around his shoulder and started to blow softly in his ear. She had a glinting jewel on the end of her tongue. Kenny wondered what it would feel like to kiss her. Looking down he could see her cleavage and her chunky breasts. Her perfume was overpowering. She was tacky, she was old, but he felt aroused all the same. He gave a weak smile and saw that Mack and Spenser were chortling at him. The woman planted a wet kiss on his cheek and left with her mate.

They went back to the club twice in the following weeks.

Kenny liked it there. Because he was with Mack and Spenser he could sit back and watch. He had nothing to prove. On the third night Spenser started to talk to a woman at the bar and then disappeared. Going to the toilet Kenny saw him in the corner of the chillout room, half-lying on one of the settees with the girl, his hand under her top.

Wasn't he married?

As they were about to leave Spenser asked Mack for the car keys. Mack held them out with an exaggerated sigh. They were using Mack's car for sex. It gave Kenny a funny feeling.

"He won't be long. Ten minutes tops!" Mack said.

Mack and Kenny went outside to a small mobile café a few metres away. While they queued for tea Kenny noticed a poster stuck on the side of the café. There'd been a similar one in the entrance of the Sugar House but Kenny's eyes had swept over it. It was a police poster. The words *Suspicious Death* were at the top and a small passport-type photo of a young man. Mack saw him looking. He picked up two polystyrene cups of tea and walked away from the counter towards an archway that was out of the cold.

"Some kid ended up in the water a week or so ago. After the club had shut. Probably drunk, or doped." Mack shrugged, glancing at his watch.

"Dead?" Kenny said.

"Freezing water. Heavy clothes. Inebriated. Not a good combination at two o'clock in the morning."

"Is that what time it happened?" Kenny said.

"I don't know! I wasn't here. Probably. Look, there's Spense."

Across the quays Spenser was walking towards them. The girl had peeled off and was heading for the entrance to the club.

"Well," Mack said, "did the earth move for you?"

"Where's my tea!" Spenser laughed.

One night, a few days later, Mack called for him unexpectedly.

"Quick," he said, walking away from Kenny towards his car. "There's someone I want you to see."

Kenny got in.

Mack started to talk about Spenser almost straight away. "Spenser can't come out to play tonight," he said in a singsong voice. "His wife won't let him. Look at him. House, kid, the lot. He's up to his eyeballs in debt. And what does he get? One shag a week if he's lucky."

Kenny didn't say anything. Talking about Spenser had made Mack edgy.

"I offered to help Spense out. Give him a loan. He

won't hear about it, though," Mack said, going off in a different direction. "He wants to support his *own family*."

"Where we going?" Kenny said.

"Do you know how much debt Spense is in?" Mack said. "He's got thirty grand owing on credit cards. *Thirty grand!*"

Kenny sighed. He let Mack talk on.

"There!" Mack said, suddenly, pulling the car over. "There, look!" he said, pointing to a fast-food shop.

Kenny looked. It was dark but the shop was brilliantly lit from the inside and the counter and serving staff could be clearly seen. There were two people serving and one customer pointing at the wall-mounted menu.

One of the staff was Jon Tibbs. He was staring out into the darkness, his elbows on the counter. He had a red uniform cap on but his face, his small round glasses, were unmistakable.

"See? There's your nemesis!"

"Hardly," Kenny laughed. "How did you find him?"

"I saw him down the pub. He was getting dope from this bloke I know. Tommy, you know him. Funny bow tie. Tommy Fortune."

Kenny nodded.

"So I followed him here. I've had him under surveillance for the last few days."

Mack said it proudly and Kenny turned to look at him, astonished. He *followed* Jon Tibbs? Didn't he have better things to do?

"You owe him one," Mack said, as the sound of his mobile ringing filled the car.

As Mack answered the call Kenny thought about it. He did "owe" Jon Tibbs. He wouldn't forget that night on the platform. In front of Nat. If Mack hadn't come along he might have been badly hurt. He took another look at the fast-food restaurant. Tibbs was laughing with his fellow worker and Kenny felt a mild stirring of annoyance.

Mack's voice had got louder. Kenny turned to look at him. There was a change in the atmosphere in the car. Mack had tensed. The tone of his voice was different: *What? When? No!*

"What's up?" Kenny said as Mack slammed the lid of his mobile.

"Spense has been arrested. He's in custody!"

"Where? Why?"

"I'm just telling you what I know!" Mack said. "The police picked him up an hour ago. I don't know any more than that. Spenser's been nicked!"

They sat in silence. Kenny was looking out at the fast-food shop. Mack was banging his knuckles together, swearing under his breath.

Jon Tibbs was cleaning his glasses.

The next day Mack phoned him and told him what had happened. Spenser was on remand in a prison in Kent. He'd been caught stealing from the cargo warehouse at Stansted. He beat up a security guard who happened on him in the loading bay. He was seen running away by a member of the public and filmed by a CCTV camera. His case wouldn't come up for months. Spenser would get real prison time, Mack was certain.

Prison. Stuck in a cell for twenty-three hours a day. Mixing with murderers and rapists. Leaving his family behind.

What could be worse than that? Mack said.

NINETEEN
NATALIE

Natalie and Joe sat for a few moments in the stationary car. The heater was on and she sank into the warmth. The radio was low, a talk station, just what Joe liked. Natalie preferred music.

"How are you?" she said, politely. "How's uni?"

"Good," Joe said, firmly, a slight cough afterwards.

"The course going well?"

"OK," Joe said, a hint of uncertainty in his voice.

"You think you might know where Kenny will be?"

"Yes," he said with a small cough. "There's an all-night café in Poplar. I used to go there with him. He likes it. Just along the A13 and then off at the crossroads."

"How long will it take—" she started.

"Nat, we should talk. I think everything's happened so quickly... We never really had a chance to go through it all."

Natalie didn't speak. Joe wanted to go through it all.

As if it was an essay that he could redraft. Analyse it, explain it, boil it down to a number of key points. How could she explain what happened?

"I know that when I went to uni I probably expected too much. Leaving you alone. It was a lot to ask. If I know Kenny he probably just tried to keep you company. I mean Kenny's immature. He probably thought he was doing me a favour by looking after you. The pair of you got too close. I can understand that. Maybe you mistook feelings of friendship for something else. It's not too late to put it right."

It was a nice picture. Her and Kenny drawn to each other by accident, because Joe was away. It was a long way from the truth. She'd wanted Kenny for weeks before Joe went to uni. Should she tell him that?

"We could try and forget it all. Go back to the way things were," Joe said.

She took her gloves off and fiddled with them, matching the fingers up as if she was going to put them away in a drawer.

"I don't know exactly how it started," she lied. "But I'm a bit too tired to talk about it now. Could we just find Kenny? Maybe me and you can talk about it tomorrow."

"OK," he said, cheerfully.

He put his indicator on and moved slowly away from the kerb.

"It's not far," Joe said. "Five, eight minutes tops."

She looked sideways at him. His hair was tied back in a ponytail. She glanced around the car. The back seat was full of his books and box files. On top were a couple of rolled-up posters. Probably some campaign or other that he was involved in.

What had drawn her to him? His passion for changing the world? It had been fun at first, but as time went on it had worn her down. Too many good causes, too many campaigns. She had lost interest.

They turned on to the A13 and rode along the dual carriageway. Off the road she could see the muted lights of East London twinkling across the horizon. How many people were up, at this hour? Not many. Nat looked at her watch. It was four thirty. Not long until morning. There was some traffic, surprisingly. Joe seemed to speed up a bit because they overtook a lorry that was trundling along, looking as though it was heavily weighed down. She looked back and saw that it had Christmas lights strung across the inside of its windscreen. Ahead she saw that the snow was wafting towards them, melting as soon as it hit the windscreen. It gave her a festive feeling. She suddenly thought of Christmas and it perked her up. It would be all right. This thing with Jimmy Mackintosh would be something and nothing.

"What's Kenny been up to? Has he got himself in with a bad crowd?" Joe said, reaching across to turn the radio off.

"There's this older bloke that he goes out with now and then."

"When he's not with you," Joe said, in an upbeat voice, as though it was a good sign that Natalie and Kenny weren't together all the time.

"He sees him quite a lot. More lately," she said.

Since his birthday, ten days before, he'd been with Jimmy Mackintosh a lot.

"And it's him who's making threats?" Joe said.

"Yes. Kenny was in a fight of some sort tonight and he wouldn't go to the hospital, and then there's all these messages, one after the other, saying he has to meet this guy at the Sugar House by six. I don't know. Something's wrong. It hasn't really been right for a while. . ."

The indicator was on again and the car moved into the slip road. Natalie saw a sign for Poplar, and in the near distance, looming up out of nowhere, the giant office blocks of Canary Wharf.

They drove into some back streets and Joe parked the car. Natalie looked out and saw the place. JACK'S ALL-NITE CAFÉ. The lights were on and there seemed to be a number of people there. She got out of the car and closed the door gently. The pavement was busy, some men outside a minicab place smoking, hugging themselves because of the cold. Natalie walked past and into the café. She held the door open for Joe, who was just behind her.

There were ten or so people in the café, scattered amongst the tables. In the corner, sitting alone, was a strange-looking older woman with pink hair and a crutch leaning against her seat. Behind the counter a small man was looking intently at a Sunday newspaper.

"Hi Maurice," Joe said.

"Hello, Joe! How are you?"

"Ask him!" Natalie said.

"Have you seen Kenny, my brother?"

The man nodded.

"I have. Haven't seen you for a while though. You at university?"

"Durham."

The man put the paper down and looked interested. Natalie felt her irritation growing.

"What's it like there?" he said. "Only my son considered it as a second choice—"

"Where's Kenny?" Natalie blurted out. "We need to find him. Do you know where he went?"

The man frowned for a moment and put his pencil and paper down.

"I did see Kenny. Came in earlier. Looked a bit rough I have to say. Then he went. I got no idea where he went. People come here to buy food and drink, not to be cross-examined on their plans."

"Sorry, I just thought you might know."

"He said he might go somewhere called the Sugar House. Any idea where that is?" Joe said.

"Yeah, new club opened down West India Quays. The kind of place that puts people like me out of business. Open all night. Loads of kids descend on it after the pubs have shut."

"Why's it called the Sugar House?" Joe said, looking puzzled.

"Built it in the basement of an old sugar beet warehouse. That's the docks nowadays; shops, offices, apartments, leisure facilities. No room to unload any ships any more. Now can I get you anything. Tea, coffee?"

"We should go. See if Kenny's down at this club," Natalie said.

She walked off. Behind she heard the sound of the man and Joe talking. She walked out of the café, and stood waiting in the street, her feet stamping on the pavement, her breath in little clouds. Joe joined her a moment later.

In the car Joe started the ignition.

"We'll have a talk," he said. "Tomorrow. Anyway, I've still got your house keys. I need to return them."

She nodded and looked out of the window as they drove towards Docklands, the giant glass building of Canary Wharf like a beacon in the night.

Her house keys. She'd forgotten that he had them, had had them since the summer. Her mum and dad had been on holiday and she'd been working late and wanted to go out with her friends. She'd given him the spare keys so that he could feed the cat.

She'd never taken them back from him.

Joe had arrived home from uni on the morning of Kenny's birthday. It was a surprise visit. It was so close to the end of term they'd thought he wouldn't bother.

Kenny had told him the truth. Just like that. *Me and Nat are together*, he'd said.

After the row he came directly round to Natalie's. It had been awful. Joe had cried, he said. It had made Natalie squirm with guilt and embarrassment. Her parents were out so they went up to her room. Kenny seemed stunned, as though he'd had no idea how Joe

139

would take it. Did he think that Joe would just shrug it off? How stupid was that?

In the end she sat on the bed, clinging to him, her arms circling his chest. He turned and kissed her, softly at first and then, as though remembering his brother's distress, he held her arms tightly, so tightly that they hurt. Then he buried his head in her neck. She thought he was going to cry but he didn't.

It's done now, he'd whispered, lying back on the bed and pulling her with him. His face was strange, his eyes hooded, his mouth open. Without another word he unfastened her clothes and rolled on top of her.

Neither of them heard the door open.

When Kenny fell away from her Natalie saw Joe standing at her room door. In his hands were her keys. She froze. After a second Kenny turned round and saw his brother. Joe's face was stone. Without a word he turned and walked away. Kenny swore. He sat up and pulled his clothes on. He didn't speak, he hardly looked at her. Then he left.

It had happened ten days before and Natalie could remember the awful moment when she saw him there. Joe, her ex-boyfriend, staring at her, a look of horror in his eyes. She was laid out before him, undressed, her pale skin cold under the bedroom light, her promises and lies exposed.

"Here we are!" Joe said, cheerfully, his voice breaking into her thoughts.

She should have told him herself.

They were in the middle of Canary Wharf, parked beside an office building, the roads around them empty.

"Where's the club?" she said, looking round.

"West India Quays. It's just round the corner," Joe said. "I thought we'd stop for a moment because there's something I need."

He leaned towards her. She shifted to the side thinking that he was going for the glove compartment. Instead he turned his face to her and started to kiss her on the mouth.

It startled her and for a moment she did nothing. Then she shook her head and made noises in her throat. He kept going though, his mouth moving gently from one side to the other. When his hand rested on her breast she made a loud noise and used the flat of her hand to push against his chest.

He backed away.

"Don't!" she said.

He looked crestfallen. He blinked his eyes a couple of times. It was as if he'd just seen her all over again, lying on the bed with his brother. She turned her face away, moving apart from him, to the passenger side of the car.

Then he started the engine up and they drove on.

TWENTY
SUNDAY, 18 DECEMBER, 5.12 A.M.

Docklands loomed up in front of Kenny, the lights from Canary Wharf stark against the black sky. It seemed close enough to reach out and touch, but in fact it was a five-minute drive, cutting through back streets, going round roundabouts, on to the dual carriageway, through an underpass.

A beeping sound made Tommy undo his greatcoat and fish out his mobile. For a few moments he scrolled through a message. Kenny looked away, out at the DLR, which was deserted, the trains sitting waiting for the morning start. He suddenly saw himself, an hour or so hence, standing on the station of West India Quay waiting for an early train on his way home after the meeting with Mack. It gave him a curious feeling, an unpleasant tickle in his ribs. A hour was only sixty minutes. A compact and finite amount of time. But the things that could happen in an hour were huge and ongoing. They could last a lifetime.

"Be there soon," Tommy said, breaking into his thoughts.

Kenny nodded.

The cab turned off the dual carriageway towards the docks. Directly in front of them was Canary Wharf, thousands of lights and miles of glass, rising up like a giant lighthouse. For a few moments they seemed to head towards it, then they took a sharp right. They lost sight of the office blocks and found themselves in the shadow of a building site, the legs of huge cranes squatting on the road so that they had to zigzag to get round them. Further on it was clear and they slowed down for sharp speed humps and sailed past skips and huge bins on wheels. Then they turned into a long road that edged on to the old docks. On one side were brick-built warehouses, most of which had been turned into apartments. On the other side of the road were moored boats and beyond those the black waters of the docks.

Looking out of the cab window Kenny could see that the area appeared to be deserted. Up ahead was the glow of the purple neon lights of the Sugar House. As they got closer he could see the tiny coloured lights of a giant Christmas tree that was on the edge of the building site next door to the club. There was some movement as well, a couple of cars pulling away, a knot of people smoking, a couple kissing passionately at the door of the club. A feeling of apprehension took hold of him.

Here he was.

"Go past," he said to the cab driver. "Past the club to the café."

143

Tommy got his wallet out of his pocket and began to sort through it.

"I'll call the guy with the iPods. He'll come along as soon as he knows we're here. . ." Kenny said.

Tommy nodded agreeably. He tweaked the bow at his neck. Kenny got a ten-pound note out of his pocket and held it out so that the driver could take it without turning round.

"Keep the change," he said, getting out of the cab.

In front of them was the café. It was quiet. A few people had taken their drinks and food and sat on the wall of the quay or stood under the brick arches of the derelict warehouses that were waiting to be made over into modern apartments. He and Mack had done the very same thing some weeks before.

As the cab drove away Kenny headed for one of the archways and stood back, out of sight and out of the freezing air that seemed to roll off the water. He turned down the offer of a sandwich as Tommy strode off to the counter.

He got out his mobile and began a text. *Mack. . .* he started and then continued for a line. It wasn't right though, so he deleted it. A feeling of anxiety snaked about inside him. He had to keep calm. He looked up to see Tommy returning. He had a paper plate in one hand holding half his sandwich. The other half he was eating. He went back to his mobile.

I'm outside the Sugar House with T. I'm not bringing him unless we talk first.

He pressed the *send* button.

"I'm thinking of opening a café," Tommy said, chewing his sandwich with relish. His swollen eye looked purple under the glow of the neon lights. "Making tea and sandwiches. You know, going straight. Making a living without having the law breathing down your neck."

"Why don't you?" Kenny said.

"I might. I've got some serious money coming to me so it might happen."

A flashing blue light took Kenny's attention away. It was moving down the road that they had come along minutes earlier. He was expecting to see a police car but it was unmarked, the light on top flashing ominously. Moments later it pulled up outside the main entrance of the club.

"What's that all about?" Tommy said from behind.

The door of the car opened and a couple of men got out. Plain-clothes policemen, Kenny thought. Someone came from inside the club and began to talk to them. What was happening?

"See that tall one with the bald head. That's Sullivan. He's the one who's always after me," Tommy said, hissing into Kenny's ear. "He can't see me round here."

"He's not here for you," Kenny said, edging back, into the archway. "Something's happening in the club. They'll be gone in a minute."

"He's not a nice man."

"Just stay calm. It's probably to do with drugs or maybe the kid who fell in the water a while ago."

But Kenny felt a moment's panic. Could it be that they

were after Mack? That Mack had been found out? That maybe the police had got information from some other source? A CCTV image? A camera that neither he nor Mack had noticed.

After a few tense moments the doors opened and the detectives reappeared. They were alone and talking loudly, one of them laughing. Kenny felt his breath easing quietly out of him as the car doors slammed and the engine started up and began to move towards them.

"Mr Sullivan mustn't see me here!" Tommy said.

"Just stand back," Kenny said, and edged further back himself.

The car moved past them, its light still circling, throwing a veil of blue across them for a moment. From inside Kenny could hear the sound of a radio. He stood still, his face wedged against the brickwork. He could feel the heat of Tommy's body behind him.

The car stopped at the café and its window slid down. Some words were exchanged but Kenny couldn't hear what was being said. The man in the café passed something into the window. Sandwiches. That's what it was. The detectives were hungry. A few moments later two white polystyrene cups followed.

Kenny relaxed. They weren't after Mack.

"They've gone," he said.

He turned round. There was no one behind him. Tommy had moved. Kenny's eyes scanned the darkness of the building, the corners and doorways. He listened hard for any sound of footsteps or breathing. But there was nothing. He walked back ten metres, looking into the darkness. He gave a low call, "*Tommy!*"

There was no sign of him. Just then there was an insistent beep from his mobile. He pulled it out. It was a text from Mack.

I'll be across the bridge where we were this afternoon. We can talk. Bring T with you.

Kenny looked hopelessly around. He'd lost Tommy.

TWENTY-ONE
BIRTHDAY PRESENT FROM MACK

On the day of his birthday Mack sent a text.

Got a great idea for your birthday present. See you later.

In the afternoon he went with his dad to pick up the new mobile. When they got back he saw his brother's Ford parked outside the house.

"I didn't know Joe was coming home."

Kenny got out of the car and paused on the pavement. It would be the first time he had seen Joe, face to face, since starting things up with Nat.

"Coming in?" his dad said, at the front door.

He looked at the Ford. He knew what he had to do. It was simple. He had to tell his brother the truth.

Joe was in the kitchen, sitting at the table, eating a fried egg on toast. The room was hot and Kenny pulled his jacket off and let it flop over the back of a chair. From behind he could hear his dad going upstairs.

"What's up?" Joe said brightly, cutting a square of toast topped with egg yolk.

148

Kenny noticed the present. A DVD-sized box wrapped in red paper, its edges crisp, a label at the corner, the name KENNY written neatly on it. How typical of Joe to do it properly, wrapping paper, label. There was probably a tasteful card somewhere. This was stuff Kenny had never been very good at. His presents were often late and offered up in the carrier bag in which he'd bought them. His cards non-existent. Joe saw him looking at it. He smiled and then went back to his egg on toast.

Kenny had to tell him. It was the right thing to do.

"There's something you should know," he said. "About Nat and me."

Joe stopped eating and looked expectantly at him.

Later, when he was in Nat's bedroom, lying on top of Nat, his clothes half on and half off, he remembered the DVD, perfectly wrapped, his name in the corner.

The room was in twilight. The lamp on Nat's bedside table throwing a thin yellow glow over the bed but leaving the rest of the room in darkness. Kenny felt tired. He looked at the bedside clock. The numbers stared sullenly back at him. 6:58 p.m.

"Are you thinking about Joe?" Nat said.

What had he done? His brother's face, so *stunned* when he told him. Had he expected it to be different? That Joe would shrug his shoulders and say, *OK, you have it*, as if Nat were some kind of toy that Joe wasn't bothered about any more? He closed his eyes. For a moment he felt them swimming with tears but he held his eyelids fast and pushed his head into Nat's neck as she tightened her grip on him.

He felt the door open. Even though he wasn't looking he sensed the air moving across his back. The room had become cold. Below him, Nat had stiffened, the only movement was her chest rising and falling.

He edged away and turned round.

There was Joe. Standing in the doorway of the room. He stared at them, his eyes flicking from Nat to Kenny, Kenny to Nat, his mouth open in what? Shock? Astonishment? Rage? Then, in the second it took for Kenny to blink, Joe was gone, his footsteps on the stairs, the front door slamming from below. Nat stood up first. Kenny grabbed his shoes and pulled them on, fastened his buttons, pulled on his sweatshirt.

Nat's face was written over with misery. She was holding the sheet in front of her as if she didn't want Kenny to see her any more. She held her hand out to him but he shook it off and grabbed his coat, leaving her there, on her own.

Out in the street he came to a full stop. Joe had already gone. He stood hopelessly. It was a mess, the whole thing a complete and utter disaster. He should go home, face up to it. A beeping sound came from his pocket. His mobile. He took it out. There was a message from Mack.

Meet me at nine at the Huntsman in Epping. I should have your birthday present by then. Don't be late. Mack.

Mack's timing was rich. His *birthday*. The importance of this day had sunk like a stone amid the events of the afternoon. He set his mobile on *silent* and began to walk.

A while later he was on the high street, his hands in his pockets, his head down. He had no idea where he was going and was walking in a straight line, forcing other people to step around him. There was a sharp wind which seemed to smack him in the face every time he turned a corner. Up ahead he could see the sign for McDonald's. He headed for it, sorting in his pockets for coins.

His mobile vibrated. It was a call. The word MACK was on the screen. He was tempted to let the answerphone pick it up but he didn't.

"I'm in Poplar. I can't get up to Epping now," Kenny said, sullenly.

"Get the tube, mate. I promise you'll love my birthday present."

"I'll never get there for nine."

"You will! Get the tube to Epping. It's a ten-minute walk. You sound miserable. What's up?"

"Some girlfriend stuff. . ."

"She not putting out for you, mate? Never mind. My present'll cheer you up. Don't let me down now!"

The call ended. Kenny looked around at the dark street. He could go home or go back to Nat's. Neither thought appealed to him.

Why not go and see Mack?

The walk from the tube took just over fifteen minutes. Approaching the pub he stopped for a moment to catch his breath. He got his inhaler out. He hadn't used it for hours and felt his chest tightening. He leaned on a garden wall and inhaled. Then he walked on. Just as he was about to turn into the pub he saw Mack walking towards him down the road that came from the forest. Mack gave him a wave, and waited, and in a moment he was there beside him.

"All right, mate?" Mack said, his cheeks rosy, looking out of place on foot instead of in his car.

"Where's the motor?" Kenny said.

"I had to park up a bit." Mack gestured back up the road.

Kenny went to push open the pub door when Mack stopped him.

"No, let's give you your present first. Follow me."

Mack turned and walked briskly away from the pub, towards the forest. Kenny paused. He felt like a drink. He felt like a sit-down in the warm pub. He didn't feel like walking any further than he already had.

"Mack," he said.

But his voice was half-hearted and he started following Mack away from the pub towards the darker end of the street. Part of him was irritated, but he was also becoming mildly curious about Mack's idea of a birthday present. Whatever it was, why hadn't he brought it round his house?

Thinking of his house pulled him up sharp. What was happening there? Were his parents comforting his brother? The thought of it made him squirm. Up ahead Mack was slowing and looked as though he was turning off the road, down a track somewhere. Kenny stood still for a minute and gave a deep sigh. He should never have come. There was something odd about this twenty-five-year-old bloke wanting to be with him. Nat thought so; Russell thought so. He almost turned there and then but Mack was calling to him. He walked on. This would be his last night with Mack. He'd get the gift, whatever it was, and go. After this he wasn't going to be available for Mack any more. He'd go home and face up to the music.

Make a fresh start. Him and Nat. All out in the open.

The lane led up into the forest. He recognized it from the time when they'd driven Mack's car up there. There were no streetlamps and it was pitch dark, just an odd light from the houses whose gardens backed on to one side. On the other side stood the thick trees and bushes of the forest, inky black.

Mack's car was parked half on the verge and half on the road. It had its back to him and he could see the shape of a head in the back seat. Someone was sitting in there. Mack had stopped and was hanging on for him so he quickened his step. Better to get whatever it was over and done with. The presence of someone else in the car made him feel better for a second. Maybe he could take the gift and shoot off, leaving Mack with someone else to drive round with. A new mate, someone to replace Spenser.

"I brought him here," Mack said, excitedly, gesturing towards the car. "He thinks I've gone off to pick up some dope. Fortune passed him on to me." Mack was breathless from walking along the road. "He won't know it's you at first, so just get in the passenger seat and don't turn round for a minute."

Kenny had no idea what Mack was talking about. He didn't bother to ask for an explanation. He opened the door and got in at the same moment as Mack. The car doors seemed to shut exactly together.

"This is my mate, Kenny. He's got some good stuff," Mack said, turning the ignition and starting the car.

Kenny turned round. A face looked at him from the back seat as the car pulled away from the verge and accelerated towards the forest. It was Jon Tibbs.

"I don't get it," he said to Mack.

Jon Tibbs swore. "What's he doing here? What about my dope?"

"That's your birthday present." Mack smiled, moving faster up the lane, the trees whizzing by, some branches and leaves reaching out and slapping the car as it went past. Kenny frowned.

"Where we going?" Jon Tibbs said. "What about my stuff?"

"You owe him one, Kenny! I'm going to see you get a chance to do it," Mack said.

Without indicating Mack took a sudden turn to the left and went down a narrower lane. He accelerated and the car seemed to shoot away, the headlights illuminating the track ahead, only thick darkness on each side.

"Mack, this is stupid," Kenny said, "I don't care that much—"

The noise of the car screeching to a halt stopped

Kenny mid-sentence. He fell forward and just stopped himself hitting the dash. "*Whoa!*" Mack said. Jon Tibbs cried out. It looked as though he'd hit his face on the back of Kenny's seat. His hand was over his nose.

"Come on," Mack said. "Here's your birthday present!"

His mind was racing. What did Mack mean? They seemed to be in a clearing. A parking area. Jon Tibbs had thrown the back door open and was scrambling out of the car. Mack sprung out, quicker than him, and stood in front blocking his escape.

"Come on, Kenny, get out. Here he is. The Big Man from the station. Three against one, wasn't it? We're giving him better odds than those he gave you. Here it's only two against one!"

Kenny got out and walked round the car. The ground was uneven and they were surrounded by dense bushes and trees. The headlights of the car sent a beam of light into the blackness.

Jon Tibbs was standing out in the middle of the clearing. He was holding his nose. Kenny could see blood coming out of it.

"What's going on?" he said.

Mack took two strides forward and shoved him. Jon Tibbs stumbled backwards, falling to the ground then scrabbling to get back up on his feet. When he was standing he was on the edge of the car lights. His expression was one of bewilderment, looking first at Mack then at Kenny.

"Don't you remember, mate?" Mack said, his voice

louder. "That night on Stratford station. When you and your pals picked on my mate here. Three against one."

"I don't remember. . ." Jon Tibbs said.

He did remember. Kenny saw a flicker of recognition pass across his face.

"You're Joe Harris's brother," he said.

Kenny nodded. He looked at Mack who was standing with his legs apart, slightly crouched as though he was a fighter in a ring. He looked ridiculous. The whole thing was ridiculous. He turned back to Jon Tibbs and was surprised to see that he'd taken his glasses off. He felt a stirring of anger, remembering that night when Tibbs had taken his glasses off to give him a kicking. He had a right to be angry. But this . . . this was *ridiculous*.

"Mack, this is. . ." He held his hands out.

Mack lurched forward. Jon Tibbs jumped backwards, his glasses falling into the darkness. He darted past Mack and stood by the back of the car. He was in shadow so Kenny couldn't see him that clearly.

"That's right," Tibbs said, his voice quivering. "You're Joe Harris's little brother. I remember that night. You put up a fight. More than your brother would have done. He still wearing his *beads*, is he?"

Mack was walking towards Tibbs. Kenny was about to bar his way, but faltered when he heard the comment about Joe.

"Joe wouldn't back off from a fight!"

He was annoyed. What did Jon Tibbs know about Joe?

"Don't mess about Kenny, have him, now, while you got the chance!"

"Joey Harris is a tosser!" Tibbs said, circling away from the car, his eye on Mack the whole time. "Everyone knows that!"

Tibbs turned suddenly and ran.

"Quick!" Mack said.

Kenny ran after him. His chest puffed up, his throat stretched and dry, his arms rigid. Away from the lights of the car it was dark. In a few seconds Kenny's eyes got used to it and he could pick out the shape of Tibbs running ahead. There was a crashing of branches and leaves and then he heard a grunt. Tibbs had fallen. He reached him in a second and jumped on his back, punching him in the ribs, pushing him down with his whole weight, riding him, feeling him squashed face down into the ground. Then Mack was behind him, he could hear his breathing, hear his feet moving across the leaves and twigs. Kenny pulled Tibbs's arm back and heard his squeal, he held it for a few seconds. He knew, if he wanted, he could break it. Just like that.

He let go.

He leaned back, stood up, found a tree to hold on to, his breath bursting out of his mouth. He was about to speak when Mack stepped past him, picked up Jon Tibbs by the shoulders, pushed him against a tree and punched him in the chest, two, three times. Kenny could hear the sound of Mack's fist hitting Tibbs, the grunt as Tibbs's breath came out.

157

He watched, his mouth open in shock, as Jon Tibbs slid down into a heap on the ground.

"What did you do that for?" he said.

"Just helping, just showing the boy what's what."

"You've hurt him."

"That's the point, Kenny!"

Mack laughed to himself and walked past Kenny back towards the car.

"We can't leave him here!"

Kenny looked at Jon Tibbs on the ground. He seemed to have lost his shape, just a bundle of clothes.

"I need a drink," Mack said.

"He might be badly hurt! We have to get him into the car!"

"He's not bleeding over my back seat. No way!"

"We can't leave him here!"

"He asked for it. You can't go feeling sorry for him now!"

Mack walked off. Kenny didn't know what to do. A moan was coming from Jon Tibbs. He hesitated and went back to him.

"Are you OK?" he said, in a loud whisper.

What was he whispering for? There was no one to hear. This was stupid. He squatted down and looked. Jon Tibbs's nose was crusted with blood. Another moan. He looked around. He could only see the distant glow of the headlamps through the foliage. He couldn't carry or drag Tibbs on his own. Why had Mack just left him there?

He walked towards the light, angry. When he got back

to the car Mack was walking up and down drinking from a can.

"I can't carry him by myself."

Mack didn't speak. His face looked different. Hard. Closed up. He was swigging from the can, one mouthful after another.

"I'm ringing for an ambulance!" Kenny pulled his mobile out of his pocket.

"Don't," Mack said, testily. "I've got a blanket in the boot. Get it out and spread it on the back seat."

He threw his car keys. Kenny caught them with a sense of relief. Now they could get away from here, drop Tibbs off at A & E.

Opening the boot Kenny rummaged around. The rear lights gave off a glow that meant he could just about see what was in there. It was full of stuff and he moved a bag and a box to find the blanket. When he pulled it out something came with it. A shirt. A white shirt. He went to replace it when he saw dark stains across the middle of it. Distracted he pulled it close to the light. The stains were brown, thick brown, rusty.

The bloody shirt. The one Mack had worn when the black kid was stabbed. Here it was, in his boot, years later. Spenser had told him but he'd hardly believed it. A trophy, he'd said.

"Come on!" Mack said.

Kenny pushed the shirt back into the boot. This was not the time to be sidetracked. He pulled the blanket out and handed it to Mack who spread it out.

"Come on!" Kenny said, impatient, striding out.

Mack followed him, in among the bushes and trees in the direction that they'd gone ten minutes before.

"Tibbs?" Kenny called, walking carefully, his eyes adjusting to the darkness as they'd done before.

"Jon, Jon!" Mack shouted.

Kenny was in front, sidestepping obstacles with care. How far had Tibbs come? Not this far, he thought. He could see for a couple of metres around, the shapes of trees and the undergrowth, the rocks and fallen tree trunks, the patches of clear ground. He turned back towards the car where the headlight beams gave off a ghostly sheen. This was the right direction. Wasn't it?

"It was over that way," Mack said, as if reading his mind.

He let Mack go ahead. He kept close, putting his feet into Mack's tracks. They walked for a minute, two minutes. Then Mack stopped.

"I don't get it!"

"Maybe he's legged it!" Kenny said.

Mack smiled at him. "He's pulled a fast one."

That was it. Tibbs had been faking his injuries, moaning and groaning when he hadn't been that badly hurt. As soon as Kenny walked away from him he'd got up and run.

"He's probably down at the pub by now," Mack said.

They both walked back towards the car. Kenny turned his neck from one side to the other, his shoulders loosening, his whole body relaxing. Tibbs was gone. It made him feel good. It was a stupid set-up and it was Mack's fault, but now it was over. He needed a drink and then he needed to go home and go to bed. His brother's face came into his head but he pushed it aside. He'd have to deal with all that tomorrow. He'd had enough grief for one day.

Mack walked to the driver's door and got in. Kenny went round the car, flexing his shoulders, stretching his arms as far as they would go, feeling the tension fall away from him. He put his hand out to pull the door handle and saw something out the corner of his eye.

"Wait," he said.

Just out of sight, at the edge of the clearing, on the fringes of the darkness.

A foot.

His face seemed to lock as he looked at it. He rubbed his eyes and moved a step away from the car.

"Get in, Kenny!"

There it was. Two feet lying slightly apart, their soles clear now, the haze of light from the car picking them up, the rest lying out of sight. He walked another couple of steps, holding on to the side of the car.

Then Mack was out of the car, looking at him.

"What's up?"

He could see more clearly now. Feet and legs. Mack turned in the direction that he was looking. He didn't speak. He walked across. Kenny couldn't. Inside there was a feeling of dread like thick mud in his ribs.

Mack swore. He was standing in the darkness looking down. Then he was squatting. He pushed something and looked round. Kenny couldn't move, couldn't take a step back or forward. Mack got up and marched over to him.

"He must have crawled away. . ."

But Kenny couldn't look. Mack grabbed his elbow and pulled him until he was standing looking down at a body. Jon Tibbs, his eyes wide open.

"I just punched a couple of times. . . He can't be. . ."

But he was dead. Kenny could see that.

TWENTY-TWO
NATALIE

Nat and Joe walked out of the Sugar House with the last stragglers. They stepped round a couple who were wound around each other in a deep kiss. A drunk man knocked into Natalie and apologized three or four times. The doorman looked at them quizzically.

"Find your brother?" he said to Joe.

Joe shook his head. "Thanks for letting us look."

"Maybe he left earlier."

They walked out into the night. A freezing blast of air came off the water and Natalie shivered. Joe's car was parked right outside, on the edge of the quay.

"What about a hot drink?" Joe said. "We could sit with it in the car. It's almost six. Didn't you say that those messages for Kenny said he had to be here by six? If we hang around we might see him."

Natalie nodded. She so wanted to see Kenny. To make sure he was all right. To have him there in the car between her and Joe. Maybe, she thought, hopefully, the three of them could pound it out, put things straight, bury all the bad feeling.

She touched her mouth, thinking of the kiss that Joe had put there earlier. If he saw her and Kenny together – not like before, in her bedroom – if he saw them sitting side by side, talking to each other, sharing a joke, he might see them as a proper couple and get past it.

Joe bought two cups of tea at the mobile café. They walked back to the car and got in. The tea was too hot to drink and Natalie took the lid off and blew across the steam. From their parking place they could see the front of the Sugar House and the café and the arches of the derelict warehouses sinking back into the darkness. Joe was quiet but she could feel that he wanted to talk, the silence between them like a wall he was peering over. Maybe it would be better to have it out now, to get it over with.

"When you went back to uni I was going to finish it. You're a lovely guy but you're too. . ."

"Boring?" Joe said.

"No, I wasn't going to say that. . ."

But the word was there in her head. His concerns, his interests, the things that she had liked about him at the beginning, were the things that had bored her as time went on.

"You seem so much older than me. Not in years but in your *interests*. The thing is I never said . . . you know . . . that I loved you. We never had . . . you know . . . slept together."

"You mean we never had sex?" Joe said.

"It wasn't serious for me. I'm sorry if it was for you."

"You didn't need to jump into bed with my brother."

"I was going to tell you," she said, ignoring the picture that Joe had painted. "When you rang, when I emailed you, but it seemed cowardly, doing it when you weren't *facing* me. If you'd come back. . ."

But she was lying. She knew it. She hadn't wanted him to come back. He was safely in Durham and she and Kenny were having a secret affair. While Joe was far away he was just a name. In person, in front of him, she could never have carried it on. Or could she? She didn't know.

"If you hadn't gone away I would have ended it."

"I still love you."

She gulped at her tea, feeling its searing heat down the back of her throat. She had to be straight with him.

"I can't help that, Joe. I don't love you."

"Do you love Kenny?"

"I don't know."

But she did know. She knew.

"You're a two-faced bitch. You should have told me. You kept me hanging on thinking that everything was all right."

Joe was angry. He threw open the car door and got out, chucking his drink into the water below.

"Bitch!" he said.

He kicked the car door shut and marched across the road and stood outside the doors of the Sugar House, the purple neon lights oozing around him so that she couldn't make out his face.

She looked away. Let him be angry. That's how he would get over it. Let him hate her for a while. That's what Kenny had done.

That evening, when Joe found them in her room, he'd looked at her as though he hated her. He'd left her standing, without a word, and gone after his brother.

When her mum and dad arrived back home much later she'd still been at the living-room window waiting for Kenny to come back. And then it had occurred to her. What if he never returned? What if he couldn't bear to look at her again. What then?

But he did come back. When she was lying in the dark of her room she got a text from him.

I'm outside. Let me in.

She'd crept downstairs and opened the back door. He looked awful, much worse than he had earlier in the evening. He was trembling with emotion and he hugged her as if he hadn't seen her for years. She led him upstairs to her room and tried to talk to him and he kept shaking his head. He felt sweaty, as if he'd run somewhere or been walking a long distance. She had no idea where he'd been. His jeans were mud-stained as if he'd been on the ground. *Did you get into a fight with Joe?* she'd asked but he wouldn't answer, just kept shaking his head. He was upset. He was more than upset; distraught. It was then she realized how wrong it had been. What they did. Maybe it was her fault. Maybe she had led him on.

He fell asleep on her bed and she lay beside him, her arm draped over him. She must have slept as well because the next thing she heard was her mum flushing the toilet from the loft upstairs. She looked at her bedside clock. It was 03:41. She shook his shoulder. *Kenny, wake up, you've got to go.*

Kenny pulled his coat on. *I'll see you later*, he croaked and looked out the door before he crept out and went down the stairs. She'd watched out of her bedroom window as he'd gone out the back door through the garden.

For five days she didn't see or hear from him. When he finally came round something was different about him, as though he'd lost some of his fire, as though the whole experience had drained him.

She didn't ask. She was just glad to have him back.

Natalie drunk her tea and looked out through the windscreen. The noise of the door opening made her look round. Joe was getting back into the car. A cloud of cold air came in with him.

"Sorry," he said. "I shouldn't have said that."

"No," she said, "you were right. What I did was the worst thing. Kenny wanted me to tell you right from the start but it was just easier not to. I'm sorry. You didn't deserve it."

Joe looked at his watch.

"We'll give it another ten minutes," he said. "Then we'll go."

Natalie nodded. She looked at Joe's profile and felt a stab of remorse. Joe wouldn't deceive anyone. He was right. She had been a real bitch.

TWENTY-THREE
SUNDAY, 18 DECEMBER, 5.46 A.M.

Kenny stopped looking. One minute Tommy Fortune had been behind him and the next he was gone. He'd been in and out of the arches of the old warehouses, calling for him, looking in dark corners and behind columns. He was nowhere.

Now what?

Kenny walked along by the building site, ducked in behind the café and headed for the edge of the quay. He sat down on a bollard beside a group of people standing drinking from cups and talking and laughing. They were dressed for the cold, puffa jackets, hats, gloves, scarves. Kenny could see their breath coming out in clouds when they spoke or laughed. In front, only a couple of footsteps away, was the water of the dock. It was still and black and looked as deep as the ocean.

He dragged his eyes away. It had stopped snowing. Instead there was a crisp solid cold that filled the air, making it unpleasant to move. It was better to stay still, in one place, otherwise it pushed against him, forcing its way inside his clothes. Had he ever felt so cold? Kenny pulled the string of his hood and folded his arms across his chest. His bad hand felt heavier than the other and gave him a continual ache. He'd stopped worrying about his forehead or his thigh. The pain he felt had just melded with his general dismal state of mind.

Hadn't he felt like this ever since that night at Epping?

The day after had been bad. Leaving Nat's house in the early hours of the morning he'd gone home, crept into the kitchen, got a black plastic bag from the cupboard under the sink and taken it up to the bathroom. He'd peeled his clothes off, every stitch, his jacket, shoes, everything, and put them into the bag.

Then he'd showered. He'd leaned against wall tiles and let the shower wash over him until the steam filled the room like a thick fog. He washed himself over and over. He'd got out, dried himself and went back to his room. He got dressed and put the black plastic bag inside a sports bag and went downstairs. At the hall table he was distracted. There, where he'd left it the previous afternoon, was his new mobile phone, still in its box, the booklets lying at angles. *It does everything*, his dad said, as he gave it to him. *Happy birthday, son!*

Kenny left it there and went out the front door, closing it carefully behind him. It was just after five thirty and still dark. He walked swiftly out into the square and kept going. He kept his head down and stayed on the high road until he got to the big supermarket and the recycling area. He faced giant plastic drums for bottles and papers; containers for shoes and books and second-hand clothes. In a corner, behind it all, was a pile of rubbish that people dumped because they didn't have cars that would take them to the council site. Bags of cast-off clothes or old lampshades or tinkling crockery. He pulled the plastic bag out and shoved it down the side near to an old armchair and walked away.

How easy it was to get rid of his clothes. The memory was more permanent. Indelible. Written into his thoughts.

A burst of laughter startled Kenny and made him look around and remember where he was. West India Quays. Sitting on a bollard by the water. He could have been fishing. He and Russell had done it when they were younger. Sitting for hours on end holding the rod, waiting for the tug, the pull, the sign that something had bitten.

Now he was waiting for something else.

The thin whine of a motorbike seemed to split the night. It stopped the chatter that was going on as it pulled to a sudden stop in front of the café. Kenny watched as a man and woman lifted their legs off almost simultaneously. They were dressed from head to toe in matching leather suits, red and blue and white. They kept their helmets on while standing at the counter and talking to the man who sold the teas.

Kenny pulled his mobile out and looked at the time. 05:58. Mack would be waiting on the other side of the bridge. The place where he'd hurt Kenny the previous evening. Where he intended to hurt Tommy Fortune.

A beep from his mobile showed he had a message.

I'm at the bridge. What's happening?

"Tommy's lost," he said, quietly. "And so am I."

TWENTY-FOUR
COVERING UP WITH MACK

Kenny and Mack looked down at Jon Tibbs. He was flat on his back, his eyes and mouth open. In the dark he looked like he was sleeping. The sight of him made Kenny's guts swirl around.

"We killed him. . ." Mack said.

"We didn't. . . There's been some kind of accident. . ."

"He's dead and we did it!"

Kenny felt his legs go weak. He squatted down beside Jon Tibbs's body. Behind him Mack was saying, *One punch, just one punch!*

It had been more than one punch, Kenny remembered. One minute Jon Tibbs had been standing up and the next he slid back on to the ground, the life knocked out of him. Kenny's throat tightened. He reached out and put his fingers on to Jon Tibbs's neck pulse. He was hoping for a flicker of movement, the faintest throb, a sign that life was still there.

Nothing.

He stood up. *Just one punch, one lucky punch!* Mack was saying, walking up and down. He meant one *unlucky* punch, Kenny knew but didn't say.

But Jon hadn't died straight away. That was the thing that made Kenny's knees begin to buckle, so that he had to put his hand out and grab the trunk of a tree to support himself. He had been moaning. Kenny had heard him and left him there. Jon Tibbs had crawled towards them, towards the light of the car. They'd been arguing and gone off in the wrong direction looking for him. Maybe there had been a chance to save him, but they'd thrown it away.

And now it was too late.

"We've got to get away from here," Mack said, grabbing Kenny's elbow.

"We should ring for an ambulance."

"He's dead, Kenny! We killed him. We've got to get away!"

Kenny felt himself being pulled along. Mack hooked his arm and was hauling him back towards the car.

"Get in."

It was a bad dream. Kenny got in the car and felt the door click securely beside him. Outside Mack was doing something. A moment later he got in, shoving an object on to the dashboard.

"We'll get away from here," Mack said.

Kenny sat completely still. As Mack reversed the car he looked on the dashboard. A pair of battered glasses. Jon Tibbs's glasses. It was the last straw for Kenny. As the car crept out of the forest car park he turned away from Mack and began to cry.

They drove in silence, Kenny slipping down in the seat, his face against the glass of the window. Some of the time he watched the darkness outside flash by and the rest he kept his eyes closed for a different kind of darkness. His head was crawling. He pushed his fingers into his hair, pressing down on to his skull until it hurt.

The car slowed. He opened his eyes and saw that they had pulled up at the pavement. Across the street was a café but neither of them made a move to get out. Mack had his arms across the steering wheel, his forehead resting on them. Kenny's eyes strayed to the glasses on the dashboard, a bit bent but still intact, both lenses unbroken.

"You were right, back there," Mack said. "What happened was an accident. We never meant to do any real damage, just give the kid a bit of repayment."

Kenny nodded. It was what he wanted to hear. In any case he hadn't even been bothered about the *repayment* bit. That had been Mack's idea. His birthday present.

"But it won't look like that to the law. You and me, we beat him up then he died. They'll do us for murder."

Us? *Us.* Kenny wanted to argue back but what could he say? He had been there. He had taken part. But none of it had been his idea. He had had other things on his mind. Nat and his brother, Joe. How stupid it all seemed now. How insignificant when he measured it against Jon Tibbs's life.

"We didn't mean it, right? And although we'd be prepared to take the blame for giving him a pasting, there's no way we should be done for murder!"

"But if we went to the police now? If we explained?"

"What? That we kidnapped him? Took him up the forest? Beat him up till he died?"

Mack kept saying *we*. It wasn't true, though. Kenny hadn't taken him anywhere. In some ways he had been fooled into going along, just as Jon Tibbs had. Mack was telling it as though they'd planned the whole thing together.

"I've got form, Kenny. The law will just look back on their computer. My name'll be there next to the dead black kid's. One dead kid might be an accident, but two dead kids. . ."

Kenny swallowed. He looked out of the car at the café. He could drink something now. A hot tea or chocolate, something to stop the dryness in his throat. He wanted to speak but was afraid that his voice would crack into a thousand pieces.

"So we go home and act as if nothing's happened. We didn't see each other tonight. We didn't go out together. You were not with me. I was not with you. Don't contact me. I'll call you in a couple of weeks when it's all blown over, right? The main thing is not to panic. They'll find the body, tomorrow probably. It'll be on the news. No one saw me driving him, no one saw you get into the car. We didn't go in the pub. There's nothing to link us with him. . ."

Mack stopped and looked thoughtful.

"What?" Kenny croaked.

"Tommy Fortune knows. He was the one who told Tibbs I had some dope."

There was silence for a moment. Kenny could almost hear Mack thinking. He watched his profile and then flinched as Mack reached out and picked up the glasses from the dashboard. Finally he spoke.

"I'll talk to Tommy. He doesn't know why I wanted Jon Tibbs in my car. I'll tell him I dropped him off ten minutes later. In any case Tommy Fortune is not likely to go to the police. He's got too many scams going himself."

Kenny went to speak but stopped himself. Mack wasn't really talking to him any more. He was debating something in his own head. He seemed to make up his mind and then turned the ignition on again.

"Let's go. And remember, whatever you do, don't contact me."

It was Mack who contacted him in the end.

The body was found the next day. The reports were on the national news for a while, then the local news. Kenny mostly stayed in his room. He refused to go to school, saying he was ill and wanted to be left alone. His brother had returned to Durham without saying a word to him. He didn't contact Natalie. He couldn't. His mum and dad were quiet, monosyllabic, annoyed with him about the whole business. He seemed to be living in his own world, in his room. He spent hours setting up his new mobile, learning its functions, transferring his numbers. When he wasn't doing that he was watching telly. Every now and then he cast his eye over his shelves of DVDs but he had no stomach for any of them. The rest of the time he lay and stared into space; the forest and the fight eventually forcing its way into his thoughts. The punch; the unlucky punch that must have killed Jon Tibbs. How? Had it broken a rib? Punctured his lung? He went out briefly and bought the papers, found the local news stations on the radio. None of them gave any details. Just that a young man's body had been found in a car-parking area in Epping Forest. After a couple of days they named him. *Jonathon Tibbs; a nineteen year old from Poplar*. The very sound of his name made Kenny bury his face in his pillow.

At night he sunk into a deep sleep. When he opened his eyes he sat bolt upright and looked guiltily around the room. If there was a ring on the front door he tensed, his shoulders like steel. What did he think? That the police would turn up for him? That somehow he had left his mark on Jon Tibbs. He hadn't. There was no link between him and Jon Tibbs.

With Mack it was a different matter.

On the fifth day his mum knocked on his room door.

"There's a call for you," she said. "That Mack guy you went to football with?"

Kenny frowned. He took the handset and closed his room door.

"I thought you weren't going to contact me. Why didn't you ring my mobile. . ."

But then he remembered his new mobile. He'd turned

the other one off and thrown it in a drawer. He gave Mack his new number.

"Something's come up," Mack said.

"What?" Kenny said.

"I got problems. With Tommy Fortune. He says if I don't give him five thousand pounds he'll go to the police and tell them he saw me pick up the kid."

Kenny held his breath.

"I should have known. Everything is business for Tommy. Everything," Mack said.

"Have you got the money?" Kenny said.

"I got the money. That's not the problem," Mack said. "The problem is will that be enough. Will it stop there. . ."

Kenny didn't know what to say. He thought of Tommy Fortune, in the pub, flogging this and that. Five thousand pounds was a huge amount of money for him.

"What are you going to do?"

"I'll talk to him again. I'll make sure he knows it's a one-off payment."

"Do you. . ."

Kenny was about to ask Mack if he wanted him to be there but he stopped. He didn't want anything more to do with any of it.

"I'll keep in touch," Mack said.

The line went dead. Kenny wished he wouldn't keep in touch. He wished he never had to listen to Mack again.

TWENTY-FIVE
SUNDAY, 18 DECEMBER, 6.03 A.M.

Kenny stood up from the bollard. He flexed his legs and took a deep breath. He got his mobile out and had a last look around the quay.

He blinked a couple of times. Over by the building site, under the fuzzy lights of the big Christmas tree, he saw Tommy Fortune. He had his hands in the pockets of his giant coat and looked like he was a man from a different time; a hundred years or so out of date. Kenny had butterflies in his stomach as he walked towards him.

"Where have you been?" he said.

"Just avoiding certain people," Tommy said, his finger on his nose.

The detective, Sullivan. Tommy thought that the police were his biggest worry. If he knew the truth he would feel a lot less secure standing next to Kenny.

"Are we off to see your mate? For the iPods?" Tommy said. "Only I'm feeling the cold. Brass monkeys. . ."

"I'll have to call him again. I thought you'd gone."

"I'll get a drink," Tommy said, pulling a handful of change from his pocket. "Want one?"

Kenny shook his head. As Tommy walked away he steeled himself to make the call to Mack. He had to be firm, strong, he had to be able to tell Mack what to do. In his mind he practised the words, *I don't want Tommy hurt*. The words sounded light, insubstantial. Mack would dismiss them with a shake of his head. He frowned, thought of saying it a different way: *I've made a written confession. A friend's got it. If Tommy or I get hurt my friend will post it to the police.*

Would that work? Against Mack?

He looked over at the café. Tommy was standing under the lights, leaning on the counter, explaining something to the man who was serving him. Kenny could see his bow tie. He looked a bit like a clown. A circus performer unaware that someone was standing behind him with a mallet.

He was a joke, a comic figure. Someone who everyone bought things from but no one respected.

He didn't deserve what Mack had in store for him.

Kenny made himself walk. He headed for the entrance of the Sugar House, trying to put some distance between himself and Tommy, looking round from time to time to make sure he was still in place.

He stopped just by the side of the purple neon lights. They shone on his mobile making it look like some weird computer toy. He accessed Mack's number, his fingers trembling. He had to keep calm, to keep control of the situation. The dialling tone sounded and then the answerphone clicked on. He huffed. Mack must have his mobile on silent. If he waited a moment Mack would see a missed call and ring him back.

His eye moved along the line of parked cars that sat on the edge of the quay. Further up saw a dark-coloured BMW. Moving to the left he was able to see part of its registration. It was Mack's car.

In front of it was a red Ford. There were two people in it. He frowned. He pressed the redial button to try Mack again. It rang twice and clicked on to the answerphone. He decided to send a text.

I'm coming. I need to talk.

People were getting of the Ford. Kenny looked closely. When he registered that it was Joe and Natalie he shook his head with disbelief.

He pressed the *send* button on his mobile.

Moments later Joe and Nat were standing in front of him.

"Are you all right? I was worried. You've been getting all these funny messages on your mobile. I. . . We thought you were in trouble. That's why we came," Natalie said, putting her hand out to touch him.

It was like a bad dream, all his worst moments crowding in on him. He turned away from them and looked across the quay. Tommy Fortune was standing on his own by the Christmas tree, a drink in his hand.

"I'm fine," Kenny said, drawing back, away from both of them. "Absolutely fine."

"You sure?" Joe said, gruffly, avoiding eye contact.

"Look at your hand," Natalie said. "The bandage has come off."

"It's a bit better," Kenny said, turning his swollen knuckle away from her. "It's been a funny night. You go home. I've just got to see someone. Then I'll make my own way."

"We'll wait for you," Natalie said.

"No."

"We'll wait here. Then you can come home with us."

"I'll be a while."

"It doesn't matter. Does it, Joe?"

Kenny looked at his brother. Joe grunted.

"I have to go. I'll see you later."

Kenny walked away and Nat called after him.

"Your mobile. You left it round my place. That's what got me worried. I switched it off so there should be a lot of battery left."

He took it, his fingers touching her skin. She felt warm, soft. He wished he didn't have to go. He strode away across the quay towards the place where Tommy was standing. He didn't look back.

TWENTY-SIX
CRACKING UP WITH MACK

Kenny started to write a letter. He got A4 paper from his schoolbag and wrote the date at the top. Then he put his address.

Dear Sir, he started.

Where should he start? At the pub in Epping? In the car? In the forest? Or back, months ago, on the platform at Stratford. Where did it begin? Maybe it was when he chased Tibbs, fell on him, punched him over and over.

He stopped, put the paper away, pushed the idea from his mind.

There were more phone calls from Mack.

Tommy Fortune was fine. He was happy with the money. Mack was sure that he wouldn't say anything. The next day it was different. Mack was angry. Tommy had rung him and ummed and ahhed about wanting more. Five thousand wasn't much to keep someone out of prison. Ten might be a more substantial amount. Kenny asked him if he had the money. *That's not the point!* Mack screamed before cutting the call. He rang back five minutes later and Kenny listened to him going over it. There was a long silence. Could he trust Tommy to do what he said he would do?

What choice do you have? Kenny wanted to say.

Kenny went to see Nat. She welcomed him, hugged him, kissed him. It was relief to be away from his house, away from his parents and the house phone. In his pocket his own mobile was on silent. He wanted some hours when Mack couldn't reach him. The next day he went again, for longer. Part of him wished he could just stay in Nat's room, curl up on her bed and close the door so that no one could find him. Late at night though, around midnight, he had no choice but to go home.

A couple of days later Mack rang again.

"Tommy's been arrested," he said.

"What for?" Kenny said, sitting down on the floor of his bedroom, pulling his duvet off the bed behind him and covering himself as if he was in a tent.

"I don't know what for! I been keeping an eye on him and he hasn't been around today. I asked a couple of his mates and they said the police had pulled him. Some copper called Sullivan who has it in for Tommy."

"What does it mean?" Kenny said, pulling the duvet on to his shoulders so that he could see around his room.

"Kenny," Mack said, in a low voice. "Are you pretending to be stupid or what? He's been taken in for questioning. What if he offers this Sullivan, whatever his name is, some information in return for dropping charges? Information about me, Kenny."

Kenny couldn't answer. He no longer knew what to say to Mack.

He started the letter again. He'd found the name of the police detective in charge of the case. This time he wrote *Dear DI Parsons, You don't know me but I need to tell you what happened to Jon Tibbs.*

When he finished he looked at what he'd written. It took three quarters of the page. Was that all he had to say? Could something so huge, so awful be described in so few words? He put it away again, tucked it inside a textbook, in a drawer, in his desk.

The next day Mack was happier. Tommy was out. He'd reassured Mack. It was just some enquiry about some stolen mobiles which Tommy had had nothing to do with. *He was innocent!* Mack said, laughing, sounding relaxed again.

Kenny ended the call and looked at his mobile. It was nine days since Jon Tibbs died. He didn't want any more phone calls from Mack. He wanted to forget Mack, to leave him somewhere in his past. When he went to Nat's he left his mobile at home. He wanted to be completely free of the man.

A letter came from school saying he had an interview with a deputy head, Mr Mullins, on the following Monday. His mum stood beside him as he opened it. He looked at the words with incredulity. School. It was a previous life. He had never been that good at going but now he felt that he would never set foot in there again.

"You'll have to make an effort, Kenny. I don't blame you, love. I blame someone else entirely," his mum said.

Kenny looked her with astonishment. What was she talking about? What did she know?

"I blame that Natalie Franks," she said. "I always thought she had a roving eye. You be careful. She'll do the same to you that she did to Joe."

He'd thought she'd been talking about Mack.

He went up to his room. He rewrote his own letter. He addressed an envelope, *DI Parsons*, and found a stamp. He stuck it down and put it in his back jeans pocket.

On Saturday afternoon Kenny walked along the street and the BMW pulled up beside him.

"Get in," Mack called, throwing the door open.

Mack didn't say anything else and they drove on to the dual carriageway, heading for Canary Wharf.

"Where we going?" Kenny said, after a few moments.

When Mack didn't answer he stayed quiet. There was an uneasy atmosphere in the car, as if Mack was going to lose his temper. He changed gear with force and turned the steering wheel heavily, flicking the indicator up or down in a determined way. It was just before four, almost dark but not quite, the sky a musty brown colour, the lights from cars and lorries glowing in the twilight.

They took the turn for West India Quays and drove along the narrow road that led past the Sugar House. Mack parked. He got out, pulling his jacket from the back of the car.

"What's up?" Kenny said, getting out of the car.

"Over this way," Mack said.

They went past a giant Christmas tree and a café which was closed. They walked alongside a building site and headed for a small bridge. All the while Kenny's shoulders were twitching. This was different to any of the phone calls. Something had happened and Mack was spinning it out, making it dramatic. They crossed the bridge, no more than ten steps, and walked on to a crumbling section of the old quay. On one side were old warehouses, on the other wooden narrowboats that were quietly rotting away. They looked as though they'd been abandoned years before. In between them the water was scummy, murky, as though stuff had been dumped in it.

Mack looked like he was weighing up his words.

"We've got to do something about Tommy Fortune. He's a nutter. He's the one thing that links us with this. . ."

Mack was saying *us* again. But it wasn't *us*, it was him.

"I thought you said he'd agreed to the money?"

"He wants more. Ten thousand. He keeps giving me the slip. He's messing me around. He threatened to go to this DI Sullivan. He says it'll do him a lot of good, maybe more good than ten thousand pounds. He's weighing this up. He's gonna make the most of it. He'll never let this go. He'll always be on our backs."

Kenny didn't speak, didn't know what to say, had no idea where Mack was leading.

"We'll have to stop him. Make him realize that he can't mess around with us."

"Hang on," Kenny said. "There's no *us* here. It was *you* who picked Tibbs up! You who planned it. It was nothing to do with me!"

Mack looked taken aback. He gave Kenny a long stare. Then he turned to stand side by side with him and put his arm around Kenny's shoulder. Kenny started to shake it off but Mack held firm, his fingers digging into Kenny's arm, and spoke in a low, calm voice.

"Don't think for one minute that you're going to walk away from this. You are in this as much as I am. Let's remember that you were the one who hit the kid first."

Kenny moved his shoulders sharply from side to side but Mack held firm.

"If Tommy grasses me then I'll grass you. You'll take your punishment just like I will!"

With an effort Kenny shook himself free. He was breathing shallowly, watching Mack to see what he'd do next.

"I've spent the last week following him, checking on him, talking to him. I can't do that for the rest of my life. I'm going round the bend. I've got to put a stop to it. Once and for all."

"What do you mean?"

"You find him, Kenny. Tonight. Stay with him. Think of some story to get him down here. Right here, on this dock. The best time is late, while the Sugar House is busy. Maybe really late, between four and six, when it's running down and people are going home."

"What are you going to do?" Kenny said.

"I'm going to put the frighteners on him. Maybe give him a kicking. Then he won't be so cocky."

"A kicking! What's the point? Wasn't that how it started with Tibbs?"

"Forget Tibbs. That's in the past. There's nothing we can do about that. There is something we can do about this problem."

"I'm not doing it! You do it! You don't need me."

"Tommy won't come here with me. He's not an idiot. I'd have to force him into the car and then someone might notice. This way it's simple. You bring him. I sort it out. Me and you can go on without worrying about the law."

"What about Tommy?"

Mack looked puzzled for a moment.

"Oh! Tommy'll be fine. Don't you worry about him!"

"I'm not doing it."

He turned to walk away but felt Mack's hands on his shoulders, pulling him backwards towards the empty buildings until they were both in one of the archways. He threw Kenny up against the brick wall. Kenny lost his footing and fell forward on to the ground. Mack knelt down beside him.

"Between four and six I expect you to bring Tommy Fortune here. You come on your own and call me when you're here."

"I can't! I won't!" Kenny said.

Mack dragged him up off the ground, pulled his fist back and punched him on the side of the head. Kenny felt the dull thud of the blow and staggered to the side, bright lights zigzagging at the edge of his vision, a searing pain pressing on to his forehead. Mack grabbed him before he fell and pushed him against the brickwork.

"You'll do it, Kenny. You'll do it because it's for the best. Tommy needs to know that he can't mess me around."

"I won't do it."

"You will. If you don't I'll grass you up myself and then I'll wait until you're out of prison and I'll find you and I'll finish it. You know I can do it, you know what I'm like. Spenser told you," he said, grabbing hold of Kenny's hand, pushing at his knuckles, closing his other hand across and squeezing.

Kenny cried out. He nodded. He knew what Mack was like. He remembered the bloody shirt in the boot of his car.

"Just find Tommy Fortune. Bring him here, leave him with me and I'll sort it out," Mack said, giving a final squeeze and letting go.

Kenny staggered forward. His hand felt like it was crushed. He tried to walk but the boats on the dock seemed to slide to one side and he found himself on the ground next to Mack's feet. He saw Mack's legs, the crease in his trousers, just as he had done months before at Stratford station. This time it was different. Mack lifted his foot and kicked him. He doubled up, his face on the pavement, his body burning up with pain.

Mack pulled him up and half-dragged half-marched him back across the bridge and round by the building site. He pushed him into the back seat of the BMW. Then he drove as if he were making a getaway from a crime. Kenny lay sideways across the seat, his body hurting, his hand throbbing, water running from his mouth and his nose, blood on his head. He listened while Mack detailed what he wanted him to do over and over again. Kenny blanked most of it out, his head throbbing, his hand roasting. He felt the car speed up on the dual carriageway and he slid to the side as Mack turned off towards Poplar.

With a screech, the car pulled over to the side of the road.

"I been following Tommy for the last week. There's a couple of pubs at the top of Walthamstow Market he hangs out in and a gym in Leyton he goes to. Then there's the usual places. Remember, don't tell anyone you're looking for him. Just keep your eyes open. When you find him on his own link up with him and make sure you bring him down to the Sugar House before six."

Mack got out and came to the back door. Kenny was lying in a foetal position. He flung the door open and pulled him by the shoulder so that he stumbled out of the car and fell on to the pavement.

"Don't let me down, Kenny."

Kenny's eyes were shut. All he could hear was the sound of the car pulling away.

TWENTY-SEVEN
SUNDAY, 18 DECEMBER, 6.21 A.M.

Tommy moved away from the Christmas tree, ready to go with Kenny. He patted his huge coat down. Kenny noticed flecks of snow hitting the fabric and he looked up into the sky. It was starting again, fine flakes hitting his face.

"The bloke's not answering his mobile. I said I'd meet him over there, across that bridge. It's a couple of minutes' walk. I'll go ahead to make sure everything's OK. You give me five minutes or so then you follow. Finish your drink. I should have found him by then."

"I'll chuck this and come with you!" Tommy said.

"This bloke's dead nervous, doesn't want to be seen. It's just over that way." Kenny pointed towards the far building site and the small bridge that led from it to the narrowboats beyond.

"How many iPods did you say he had?" Tommy said.

"I can't exactly remember. . ."

"You said ten. You're not trying to mess me about, are you?"

"No, ten, that's it," Kenny said.

"You're not going to go there and get them for yourself. I haven't come all this way to be ripped off."

"Why would I do that? I told you, the bloke doesn't really want anyone to see him. I'll just go over there, check he's all right and you follow me. Five, ten minutes. Drink your tea. Then follow me. That bridge, over there."

Kenny pointed to the bridge again. Only its outline could be seen. Tommy nodded, his face disappearing behind his cup.

Kenny pulled the strings of his hood and walked towards the empty building site. He was no longer registering the cold. He'd been out most of the night and his senses had finally numbed to it. Away from the lights of the tree and the café the darkness was peppered with snow. Up above he could see lights perched on cranes. The snow seemed to blizzard through their beams. Elsewhere it was gentle, festive, like on a Christmas card. He looked ahead, walking carefully, making sure he didn't trip.

On one side was the building site with its high fence. On the other was the water. Up ahead was the small bridge that linked to the dock where the narrowboats were. Somewhere over there Mack was waiting.

Kenny stepped on to the bridge. He could see the narrowboats on the other side, jet-black shapes, like silhouettes, the snow slanting across them. Walking across he wondered if he should call Mack? Or just wait until Mack saw him?

He walked on, towards the boats, passing by the arch where he had been beaten up the previous night. Anger flickered inside him. Now was not the time. He had to keep focused, to talk to Mack, to make him see sense.

Mack stepped out from one of the arches. Kenny stopped. The atmosphere was heavy, he wanted to say something to lessen the tension. He opened his mouth to speak but his eyes were drawn to Mack, to the way he looked.

He was dressed in black. On his head was a balaclava. His face looked as though he had rubbed earth or dark make-up on it. Kenny almost wanted to laugh out loud. He looked like a soldier on some kind of clandestine operation. A *warrior*. He looked ridiculous.

"Where's Tommy?" Mack said.

"I wanted to talk to you. . ." Kenny said, his words falling away.

His confidence crumbled. Mack wasn't even listening to him. He was standing completely still, only his eyes moving side to side as if he was scanning the area.

"I don't want you to hurt Tommy," Kenny said, the words coming out in a croak.

Mack smiled and walked up to him. Kenny's shoulders went stiff as Mack slung his arm around them. He'd done it the day before. It wasn't a friendly gesture.

"I don't care what you think, Kenny. I told you to bring him here. Why can't I see him?" he whispered, his mouth over Kenny's ear, his breath hot enough to burn him.

Hopeless. Kenny saw that his words would have no effect on Mack. None at all. Had he ever thought they might? Really? Or had he been kidding himself? Mack, the friendly, easygoing guy in the car who was so different from the Mack he'd seen over the last couple of weeks.

"You're useless, Kenny. You couldn't do the one thing I asked you to do."

Mack took his arm away and gave Kenny a powerful shove. Kenny stumbled and fell flat on his back, hitting his head on the concrete. In the distance he heard the sound of his name being called. Once, twice.

It was Tommy Fortune, following him, expecting to meet the man with the iPods. He tried to get up but Mack was there, his foot on Kenny's ribs.

"Sshh. . ." Mack said.

Kenny?

He could hear Tommy's voice. It was coming closer, maybe across the bridge. Kenny should call out, stop him. He tried to raise himself but Mack's foot was firmly on him, holding him down like some sort of defeated dog.

Anger flickered inside him. He struggled but Mack's boot was on his ribs and he was afraid of what the man might do. Something inside him laughed hysterically. He was on the ground again, looking up at Mack. Wasn't that what he was always doing? Hadn't it been like that since the beginning? Since that night on Stratford station?

He was Mack's puppy, to be rescued. To be played with and punished, to be petted, and bossed and reprimanded.

Kenny, are you there? Mate.

Tommy's voice was tiny. It hardly made a dent in the heavy silence. Mack put his hand in his back pocket and took something out. He inched his foot across Kenny's chest until it was over his heart. He stood rigid, like a statue, waiting for Tommy to come. Kenny looked up at his hand. Something was hanging down. It took a few seconds for Kenny to recognize it.

It was a knife.

Kenny?

Tommy's voice was louder. Kenny heard it in his head but his eyes were fixed on the knife that Mack had in his hand.

He meant to kill Tommy.

Kenny felt himself swooning, his head going light. He would have passed out if he hadn't already been lying down.

"Tommy!" he said, his voice coming from down in his boots.

"Shut up," Mack said.

You over there, mate? Tommy's voice sounded.

Mack stood back slightly, his shoulders ready, the knife in his hand, his foot less heavy on Kenny's chest. Kenny's eyes were drawn to the blade, dull and blunt-looking in the dark of the building.

Mack had lied to him, used him, tricked him. He had been weak and hopeless and now someone else was going to get killed. Deep down he felt a twist in his guts. Using all his strength he lifted his hands and gripped hold of Mack's ankle, moving it from side to side rapidly, making him unstable.

"What?" Mack whispered harshly, trying to put weight back on to Kenny.

It was too late though, he'd lost his hold. With an almighty push Kenny threw Mack off him and scrambled up as quickly as Mack toppled over. A clattering sound broke the quiet.

"Tommy, don't come round here. It's a set-up. Sullivan's here," Kenny shouted.

The knife had fallen on to the ground. Kenny stepped across and scooped it up. He held it out, his mouth open, his thoughts whirring round. Looking up he saw that Mack was on his feet, moving in his direction.

"Tommy," he shouted, holding the knife in front of him, backing away from Mack. "Tommy, don't come here. I've just seen Sullivan. It's a set-up. The police are around. Go back."

Kenny stepped backwards, holding the knife. Keeping his eyes on Mack, he glanced to the side for a split second. It was enough to see a dark figure running back across the bridge.

Mack shook his head, slowly advancing towards Kenny. Kenny stepped away, his fingers trembling, the knife moving to one side and then the other.

"You won't use that," Mack laughed. "You're soft, Kenny. You were soft that night on the station. That's why Tibbs picked on you. You're like a girl!"

Kenny looked round as he retreated, the water behind him, the old boats floating on it. Mack was shrugging his shoulders. He pulled the balaclava off and Kenny could see he was smiling. He looked like the old Mack again. Kenny glanced down at the knife.

"You were going to kill him."

Mack shrugged, taking another step towards him.

"You got me to bring him here so that you could kill him," Kenny said, stepping back, feeling the edge of the quay with his foot. He glanced round for a second and saw the old boat a step away.

"It would have solved a very big problem, Kenny. You shouldn't have interfered."

"So, what? Are you going to kill me now?"

"How could I? You've got the knife. Question is, are you going to use it?"

Kenny stared down at the knife. It was small but felt heavy, the heaviest thing he had ever held in his hand. He looked up and saw Mack, closer now, within arm's reach of him. He stepped backwards on to the boat, moving along the side, using his bad hand to keep hold of the rail, the snow cooling his skin, his other hand welded to the knife.

"Grow up, Kenny. What you going to do? Jump in the water? Swim to the other side of the dock? Just come back."

Kenny hesitated. He stared at Mack, who was standing loosely on the side of the quay, his body shaped in a kind of shrug as if he didn't really care one way or another about what Kenny did. But Mack did care. He would have killed Tommy. There was nothing to stop him doing the same to him. He had the knife but Mack could take it off him as easy as plucking an ice-cream cone from a toddler.

Kenny looked at the dark water, the snow pitting it, the lights from the tops of the cranes laying flat on it.

He had no idea what to do.

Mack seemed to be reading his mind.

"Come on, Kenny. It's all over now, mate."

Mack wasn't his mate. Maybe he never had been. Kenny made a decision. He sat down on the deck of the boat, his legs crossed. He was tired. Let Mack come and get him.

TWENTY-EIGHT
SUNDAY, 18 DECEMBER, 6.49 A.M.

In the distance Kenny could hear someone calling his name. He closed his eyes and concentrated. Inside his head the darkness was warm, tight. Outside it was untidy, dangerous, bitter cold. Mack was only a few steps away, on dry land; maybe he would hold a hand out to help Kenny off the boat.

He heard it again. His name being called. *Kenny! Kenny!* Was he imagining things? He opened his eyes. Mack was looking away from him, towards the bridge and the lights.

Kenny! Kenny!

There it was, two voices calling in tandem, coming closer.

He stood up, shakily, his leg hurting him more now, his bad hand numb, the knife jutting out from the fingers of his other hand. He was trembling with the cold. He turned to look towards the bridge and saw them. Joe out in front, Natalie behind. It occurred to him that it must be getting lighter because he could make them out clearly. They were half-walking, half-running. They got to the end of the bridge and stopped.

Kenny leaned towards them.

"Here! I'm over here," he croaked.

He stood with his back straight and glared at Mack. He held the knife up and let it drop. It slipped into the water without a sound. For a few seconds Mack looked angry. Then his face softened and he gave a little smile.

"This is a bit too crowded for my liking. Too many witnesses. Still, tomorrow's another day," he said.

Joe and Nat were on the quay.

"Over here," Kenny shouted, his voice stronger.

Mack gave a childish wave and backed off. Kenny closed his eyes, wiping the snow and wet from his face. When he opened them again Mack was gone and Joe and Nat were standing in front of the boat.

"What's up? We just saw Tommy Fortune and he said you might be in trouble. What's going on?" Joe said.

"Why are you on that boat?" Nat said. "Is it safe?"

Kenny walked towards them, grabbed Joe's hand and stepped gingerly from the boat on to the quay.

"Safer than anywhere else."

"You're freezing cold!" Joe said. "Take my coat!"

Joe pulled the zip of his jacket down but Kenny put his hand up to stop him. He'd taken too much from Joe.

He didn't tell them much, just brushed away their questions as the three of them walked back across the bridge and headed for the lights of the Christmas tree.

He was in some sort of trouble, they both knew, but neither of them seemed to want to push him.

They walked in silence. Kenny could feel Nat's fingers on his arm. Joe was further away, keeping his distance. Kenny looked at his brother's back and wished he could do something, say something to put things right.

Up ahead, near the Sugar House, he could see Tommy Fortune standing under the purple lights, his coat engulfing him, his head small and round on top of it. The sight of him gave Kenny an emotional rush. He let go of Nat's hand and speeded up. He needed to talk to Tommy.

"You all right, mate?" he said, reaching him.

"Fine, Kenny. Listen, I owe you. You saved me from Sullivan. I won't forget it. I saw Joe here and I told him you might need a hand."

Kenny looked at his brother. His hair was loose, damp with the snow. He had dropped everything to come and help him. Even after everything that had happened. He was so grateful he could have cried.

Tommy was talking, describing the detective, Sullivan. *A real devil*, he was saying. Joe was looking at his watch. It was time to go home. Kenny interrupted Tommy's flow of speech.

"Can you give Tommy a lift home?" he said to Joe.

"Don't bother. It's no problem. I'll get a cab," Tommy said.

"It's not out of my way," Joe said.

"And Nat?"

"I'm staying with you," Nat said, sharply.

"You should go with. . ."

"I'm staying!" Nat said with absolute certainty.

Moments later Joe turned the car lights on and started the engine. Kenny walked across and stood at the passenger window.

"Are you *really* all right, Tommy? I'm sorry. About the iPods."

"Don't worry about it, mate, story of my life that!"

The car did a three-point turn and went back up the lane.

Kenny stood watching until it disappeared then turned back and put his arms around Nat, hugging her tightly.

"I was worried about you. . ." she said.

Over her shoulder he could see Mack walking past the Christmas tree. He stiffened and watched as Mack swaggered across the quay and up the lane towards his car.

"What's the matter?" Nat said.

"Just stay still. Don't move."

Mack paused when he saw Kenny and Nat standing under the purple lights. Then he continued, his hand fiddling in his pocket, pulling out his car keys. From a distance he pointed his key and his car lights blipped.

Nat turned round.

"Is that Jimmy Mackintosh?" she said.

"Waiting for a lift, Kenny?" Mack shouted, getting closer.

Kenny shook his head, his arms firmly round Nat.

Mack laughed and opened the driver's door and got

into the car. He put the lights on and pulled the car out of its place in a sharp curve. Then he reversed and turned and was facing the opposite direction. He stopped, let the window go down.

"Just keep an eye out for me, Kenny. I'll be looking out for you."

Kenny didn't speak.

Mack drove off.

TWENTY-NINE
SUNDAY, 18 DECEMBER, 7.38 A.M.

It was the second DLR of the day. It was only one stop to Poplar but it felt good to be on it. Kenny pulled Nat through the carriage to the very front of the train. They sat down and Nat threaded her arm through his. She put her head on his shoulder and closed her eyes. Kenny looked out at the track ahead. The sky was grey instead of black, the shapes of buildings becoming clear. There were lights going on in tower blocks. People were getting up, making breakfast, getting hold of the Sunday papers.

Sunday was a day when Kenny usually slept late. In his room, with the blinds down and the radiator throbbing quietly under the window. He often lay unconscious until lunch time.

This would be a different kind of Sunday.

Some clubbers got on the train behind him and sat opposite each other, their voices criss-crossing in chatter. *Did you see that girl? The one Brian snogged! Yuck! She had nice hair. But that skirt. . . Brian liked her. Brian would snog a horse if there was nothing else. . . She looked like a horse. . .*

The feel of the carriage moving made him sit forward.

There was no driver. That's what he liked about the DLR. He looked through the glass as it swept along the rails like a ride at a theme park.

Would he end up in prison?

He couldn't say. Maybe. He didn't know.

Behind him the talk had turned to money. *Got twenty quid to lend us? You must be joking. . . You owe me a tenner anyway. From when? From the drinks money. . . You need to sort your finances out!*

Kenny held his hands out in front of him, his sore knuckle swollen and red. When he was a kid he used to pretend to be the driver on the DLR. To be in charge. It felt good. For a few seconds he grasped an imaginary steering wheel and pulled the train round the bend and into the station. He used his foot on a brake pedal and waited until the train had completely stopped before he pressed a button to open the doors.

Then he nudged Nat and they stood up and got off.

Outside the station it was almost light. Kenny pulled Nat across the road to a postbox. He took the letter from his back pocket. He looked at the address of Epping Police Station on the front. He had a fleeting image of Jon Tibbs. The kid with the glasses who got lost in the forest.

He dropped the letter into the mouth of the box and walked away.

10 THINGS YOU DIDN'T KNOW ABOUT ANNE CASSIDY...

1 When I was a baby I slept in a drawer for six weeks. My parents assure me that they never actually closed it.

2 I was an only child until I was fourteen. Then I had a baby brother and sister. I usually blame all of my insecurities and low self esteem on them. They're not bothered as far as I know.

3 I was one of the first people in the country to have plastic surgery on the NHS. I had my ears pinned back. When I came out of the operating theatre my whole head was bandaged up and my mum said she thought I'd had brain surgery.

4 When I was a child me and my mum and dad went everywhere together. I sat in the back of the car and sang along with all their songs. My mum was a dressmaker and made herself a dress and a miniature version of the same thing for me. I loved it as a child. As soon as I became a

teenager I hated it. My dad was a great fan of horse racing. He had a number of pens that he used to choose his horses. Some were lucky, others were not. He used to put them behind his ear for safety.

5   I went to a girls' convent high school. My best friends were the most important people in my life. Sometimes they went off with someone else and it broke my heart. I always took them back. I had no pride.

6   I was hopeless in school. I couldn't be bothered doing any work at all. I used to sit at the back of the classroom and draw profiles of beautiful women on my rough book. And sign my name over and over again. My teachers gave up on me.

7   I wore the shortest mini skirts that I could find. I also wore wigs and false eyelashes and thigh length boots. I was tacky.

8   I worked in a bank for five years. I cut coupons from bonds and presented them to other banks for payment. I sat beside a hatch window and had to open it to deal with enquiries. If I had a pound for every time someone started with *A cup of tea and a cheese roll* I'd be rich (even now, all these years later).

9 My son never reads any of my books. Even
   though he's a character in a lot of them. He
   prefers to read real life stuff about the Mafia.

10 My husband reads all of my books. He says he
   likes them but he would say that, wouldn't he?

LOOK OUT FOR MORE GRIPPING NOVELS BY

ANNE CASSIDY...

From the award-winning author of LOOKING FOR JJ

GIRL
LOST

anne cassidy

A child has been stolen...

He's out there. He's watching me. . .

anne cassidy

Love
LETTERS

From the award-winning author of LOOKING FOR JJ

Talking to
STRANGERS

Caroline got into someone's car – and now she's gone. . .

anne cassidy

From the award-winning author of LOOKING FOR JJ

From the award-winning author of LOOKING FOR J.J.

MISSING *judy*

anne cassidy

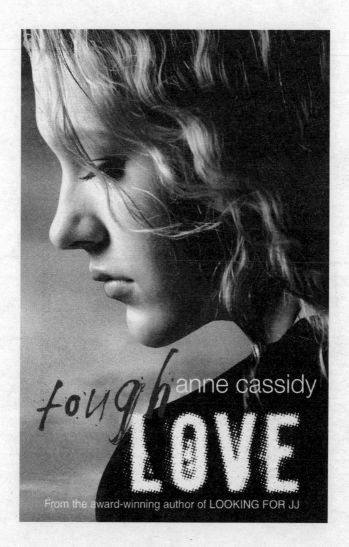

tough anne cassidy
LOVE

From the award-winning author of LOOKING FOR JJ